Sealed by a Vale

These untamed docs are almost too hot to handle!

Welcome to Crater Lake, Montana, where doctors Carson and Luke Ralston were born and raised. Big Sky Country gives these gorgeous brothers the space to leave their difficult pasts firmly behind them… until two new additions to the landscape—feisty surgeon Esme Petersen and east-coast ace Dr Sarah Ledet—upset their careful balance!

Find out what happens in

Carson and Esme's story
His Shock Valentine's Proposal

and

Luke and Sarah's story
Craving Her Ex-Army Doc

Don't miss the ***Sealed by a Valentine's Kiss*** duet from Mills & Boon Medical Romance author Amy Ruttan

Available from February 2016!

Dear Reader,

Thank you for picking up a copy of *Craving Her Ex-Army Doc*.

I've mentioned before that brothers seem to be in my cards. I love writing about brothers, and I love my little brother to death—though when we were younger that wasn't always the case. Like my hero Luke, setting booby traps for Carson from *His Shock Valentine's Proposal*, I'm afraid I was often duct taping my brother to various walls.

My mother always warned me that my brother would grow up to be bigger than me one day. She was right. He towers over my five-eleven height at six foot four. Thankfully all transgressions of childhood are in the past, and my brother is one of my best friends. Just one word, which doesn't make sense to anyone but the two of us, and we're on the floor laughing.

Carson is Luke's rock—though Luke might not want to admit it. Luke admires his younger brother, and maybe…just maybe…envies the love that Carson found with Esme in *His Shock Valentine's Proposal*.

Perhaps love is actually in the cards for lone wolf Luke Ralston, but it's not going to come easy. He's a stubborn man, and it's going to take an equally strong and stubborn woman—my lovely heroine Sarah Ledet—to tame him.

I hope you enjoy the second book in my ***Sealed by a Valentine's Kiss*** duet.

I love hearing from readers, so please drop by my website, amyruttan.com, or give me a shout on Twitter @ruttanamy.

With warmest wishes,

Amy Ruttan

CRAVING HER EX-ARMY DOC

BY

AMY RUTTAN

This is a work of fiction. Names, characters, places, locations and incidents are purely fictional and bear no relationship to any real life individuals, living or dead, or to any actual places, business establishments, locations, events or incidents. Any resemblance is entirely coincidental.

First published in Great Britain 2016
By Mills & Boon, an imprint of HarperCollins*Publishers*
1 London Bridge Street, London, SE1 9GF

ISBN: 978-0-263-26365-7

Our policy is to use papers that are natural, renewable and recyclable products and made from wood grown in sustainable forests. The logging and manufacturing processes conform to the legal environmental regulations of the country of origin.

Printed and bound in Great Britain
by CPI Antony Rowe, Chippenham, Wiltshire

Born and raised on the outskirts of Toronto, Ontario, **Amy Ruttan** fled the big city to settle down with the country boy of her dreams. Life got in the way, and after the birth of her second child, she decided to pursue her dream of becoming a romance author. When she's not furiously typing away at her computer, she's a mom to three wonderful children.

Books by Amy Ruttan

Mills & Boon Medical Romance

Safe in His Hands
Melting the Ice Queen's Heart
Pregnant with the Soldier's Son
Dare She Date Again?
It Happened in Vegas
Taming Her Navy Doc
One Night in New York

Visit the Author Profile page at millsandboon.co.uk for more titles.

For my boys. For the times you have fun together
and the times you drive each other crazy.
Remember this, Aidan, James *will* grow bigger than you.

Love you both.

Praise for
Amy Ruttan

'I highly recommend this for all fans of romance reads with amazing, absolutely breathtaking scenes, to-die-for dialogue, and everything else that is needed to make this a beyond awesome and WOW read!'

—*Goodreads* on
Melting the Ice Queen's Heart

'A sensational romance, filled with astounding medical drama. Author Amy Ruttan makes us visualise the story with her flawless storytelling. The emotional and sensory details are exquisitely done and the sensuality in the love scene just sizzles. Highly recommended for all lovers of medical romance.'

—*Contemporary Romance Reviews* on
Safe in His Hands

PROLOGUE

"GET OUT OF my OR!"

"Not on your life." Luke stood his ground. He wasn't about to be pushed out of the OR by the arrogant upstart trauma surgeon at the hospital. "I got him off the mountain and I'm not going to let him die on my watch. So if you want me out of your OR you're going to have to physically remove me."

Those blue-green eyes behind the surgical mask glittered with barely concealed rage and Luke smiled behind his own mask, knowing he'd pushed the surgeon's buttons. She was some hotshot surgeon from out east. One who had been teaching a workshop in Missoula and got called in when Shane was brought in, because Missoula was slammed.

There had been several landslides after a small earthquake rocked the area. All hospitals in a hundred-mile radius were overflowing with the injured. If Luke had the supplies he could've set up a mobile OR in Crater Lake. He'd worked in worse conditions in Afghanistan.

Only, he hadn't practiced surgery since his honorable discharge and he certainly wasn't going to start on Shane Draven. He did surgery when needed, but he preferred practicing in the wilderness. So in this situation he'd rather this trauma surgeon work on Shane.

Still, she needed to know he was just as capable as her. He would have done the surgery another way. That was why he was questioning her.

She was cocky and full of herself. She definitely needed to be taken down a peg or two and he was just the guy to do it.

He might not practice as a traditional doctor, but he was just as much a surgeon as this woman. He had spent time on the front line, patching up soldiers in the midst of fire. How many lives had he saved? He wasn't sure, because he didn't keep score. All that mattered was saving lives. That was why he'd joined the army, it was what he'd wanted for so long, but he'd given it up for another.

Don't think about that now.

This surgeon had sized him up the moment he'd rushed in with Shane Draven's stretcher. She thought he was nothing but a first responder or a paramedic. Obviously a surgeon who didn't know any better. Paramedics were on the front line.

Usually he wouldn't question another surgeon in the OR, unless the patient was at serious risk, but the moment he walked into the OR with Shane she'd been treating him like a second-class citizen. Which was why he decided two could play at that game. So he questioned her every move.

She wanted a fight? Oh, he'd give her a fight.

"I will physically remove you," she snapped.

"I'd prefer you focus on my patient, Doctor, rather than argue over my presence here."

Her angry gaze met his. "You're questioning my skill, Mr...."

Luke grinned smugly. "It's Dr. Ralston."

Her eyes widened in obvious surprise. "Doctor? I thought you were a paramedic."

"Looks can be deceiving, I guess, but I am a doctor. Though I'm not insulted you thought I was a paramedic, but I suppose that's the reason why you feel I should be kicked out of your OR."

She cursed under her breath. "Doctor or paramedic, it doesn't matter. I won't have you undermining my authority in my OR."

"This isn't your OR. You're not from around here."

"When I'm operating it's my OR, whether or not I'm from here."

Luke had to admire her spunk. And she was right. Perhaps he'd been undermining her a touch, but this was a man he'd pulled off the mountain and Dr. Eli Draven was this patient's father. He had made it clear that he was going to hold Luke responsible if Shane died, because Luke had allowed Dr. Petersen to place the chest tube.

Luke didn't know what Dr. Draven had against Dr. Petersen and he didn't really care. He'd pulled Shane down off the mountain. He was responsible for Shane's life. Dr. Draven had been throwing his weight around in the Missoula hospital, because the chief of surgery was one of his former students.

Besides, Shane was also the nephew of Silas Draven, who was sending Luke the most work up on the mountain, and Silas Draven was someone he didn't want to mess with. Luke appreciated all the work, but still he felt responsible for taking care of Shane. Luke, his brother, Carson, and Dr. Petersen were all instrumental in getting Shane Draven to Missoula alive.

Luke hadn't left Shane's side since they were airlifted off the mountain and he wasn't going to leave him now.

No man gets left behind. Every life gets saved.

Luke's commanding officer's words rang true to the credo he lived by and it wasn't going to change now. He'd served two tours of duty as an army medic. Even when he couldn't live by that credo, when life couldn't be saved, it still drove him.

Don't think about losing patients now. Not with Shane on the table.

He shook those thoughts away. There was no place for them here.

"I got this man down off the mountain. He's my patient whether this is *your* OR or not."

"If you stay, Doctor, keep your opinions to yourself, then." She looked away and continued to work on Shane. A true hardened trauma surgeon, as he'd been once.

Damn, she's a spitfire.

He admired that about her and if circumstances had been different, meaning if he had any interest in pursuing a relationship again, he'd go after a strong-willed spitfire woman like her, but she was off-limits.

All women were.

He wanted to say more, but he knew when it was best to keep his mouth shut. As long as Shane's life was saved, and then he could get Eli Draven off his back, but he still watched the surgeon like a hawk.

"Yes, Doctor." And he gave her a little salute.

The surgeon mumbled a few choice words under her breath, but continued working on Shane.

Luke tried not to move toward the side of the table, where the lead surgeon stood, because if he did that then she would have grounds to throw him out of her OR.

He might be a bit of a control freak when it came to his patients, but there was no way he'd push it any further. He wasn't leaving this OR. He wasn't going to leave Shane Draven behind.

He didn't even know her name and he didn't care; she seemed to be competent. That was all that mattered.

When the surgery was over and they were wheeling Shane to the ICU, Luke gave up his perch in the OR. He planned to be on that ICU floor and personally monitoring Shane until he came out of the woods, as it were.

Dr. Ralston is a fine surgeon and a heck of an officer.

Only that wasn't entirely true. Not anymore. He wasn't an officer anymore. He'd given it all up. He didn't renew his commission because his wife was done being an army wife, but then Christine had left him. He did it all for her and for nothing.

Luke shook that thought from his head. Nope. He wasn't going there, because he wasn't going to let that happen again.

No one was going to dictate how his life should be again. Which was why he wouldn't settle down into a practice with Carson. It had been Christine's wish after he finished his tours of duty. He'd partner with Carson, raise a family with Christine and do what he loved, practicing medicine. He'd been planning to do that. Luke was going to give up the army for his wife to make her happy. At least that had been the plan.

Then it all went to hell in a handbasket.

Christine left him when he finished his second tour, for his best friend, Anthony.

He cursed under his breath as he walked down the hall to the ICU. He was angry at himself for allowing those thoughts to creep into his head again. To let her creep into his thoughts again. It was because he was in a hospital again.

Surrounded by people.

On his mountain it was just the sky, the wind, the trees and the majestic behemoths rising from the earth toward the clouds.

On his mountain he was himself and he had no one to answer to. No one but him controlled his life, his fate, his destiny.

"Hey!"

Luke spun around and saw a woman in surgical scrubs and cap approach him. The physical attraction was immediate. Full red lips, which were slightly pouty. White-blond hair peeked out from under the scrub cap and big blue-green eyes sparkled with annoyance.

Oh. No.

It was the spitfire surgeon. He'd only seen her over the surgical mask. Now seeing that she was a gorgeous woman with a strong personality to boot, well, that was a dangerous combination for Luke.

"Can I help you?" he asked.

She crossed her arms and sized him up. "I'm looking for a Dr. Ralston. Do you happen to know where he is?"

Luke took a step back, in case she started swinging, but then the words sank in and he realized she didn't know who he was. But then, he'd been wearing a surgical mask, cap and gown when he'd been in the OR with Shane. And this surgeon wasn't a local surgeon. She was visiting. She wouldn't recognize one person from another behind a surgical mask, because not being at this hospital every day he certainly didn't.

This could be fun, one part of him thought. While the other part told him to walk away and not entangle himself with her, because he knew she spelled danger.

"Why do you need him?"

She huffed. "If you see him tell him Dr. Ledet is looking for him." She turned to walk away and for a brief moment, one fraction of a second, he saw himself grabbing Dr. Ledet and pulling her into his arms, kissing her. Forcing the image away, he overcame the urge to taste those soft, moist lips, running his hands through her blond hair.

Maybe doing a little bit more than that.

Definitely dangerous.

"Where can he find you?" Luke asked.

She glanced at her watch. "After eight he can't. I'm flying back to New York."

"New York?"

"Yeah, I was here on business and decided to lend a hand for an old teacher. A fat lot of good that did me when I had to deal with an arrogant jerk like Dr. Ralston."

"Well, if I see him before eight I'll tell him."

She didn't thank him, just nodded curtly and walked away.

A New York surgeon, eh? Well, that was too bad, but it was for the best.

He'd never see her again.

It would've never worked anyway and not because of the distance, but because he would never let it.

CHAPTER ONE

Six months later, mid-January,
Crater Lake, Montana

I HATE THE COLD. I hate the cold.

Sarah thought coming from New York she'd be used to the frigid temperatures of northwest Montana. New York State bordered Canada, too; it should be the same, but it wasn't. Not at all. This was a different kind of cold. There was no moisture in the air and as she tried to shake the remnants of bone-chilling frigidity from her brand-new office, she couldn't remember why she'd decided to take this job in Crater Lake, Montana.

Dr. Draven.

Right. Her teacher from medical school. Dr. Eli Draven. She didn't study under him, because she didn't have an interest in becoming a cardio-thoracic surgeon, but she remembered him clearly from her days at Stanford.

He was a good teacher, if not a bit full of himself. He'd taken a shine to her until she'd decided not to pursue cardio; then she was no longer his star, but he still spoke highly of her and when this job was offered to her by Dr. Draven's brother, she couldn't pass up the opportunity, because she was more than ready to get out of New York and out of her father's iron grip.

No matter what she did, nothing was good enough for her parents.

They still saw her as their baby.

And they wouldn't be happy until she was living a pampered life in a Central Park West penthouse, married to an investment banker or a lawyer or even a doctor.

She couldn't be the doctor, however.

That was unacceptable.

Why do you need to work, pumpkin? Your husband, if you marry well, can take care of you.

Her mother's archaic way of thinking made her shake her head. Sarah peeled off the thick parka she'd bought when she moved out to Montana and hung it on the coat rack in her office. There were no cabs in Crater Lake, unless you counted the very unreliable Bob's Taxi, and she didn't.

At least she'd bought a car when she first landed in Missoula and had snow tires put on it. She was well versed in the rugged country living she was immersing herself in, even if she did complain about the cold just a bit.

Why do you want to go work out in the wilderness?

Sarah's sister, who was married to a very prominent surgeon and occupied one of those coveted penthouse suites on Central Park West, couldn't understand what was driving her to do this.

Sometimes Sarah wasn't even sure herself.

Because your dad got you your prestigious appointment in that Manhattan hospital. It wasn't you.

Sarah sighed when she remembered. After a summer of touring around different hospitals in each state, presenting her Attending's research and teaching different surgeons on using the newest model of robotic surgery, she came home to New York to accept one of the most prestigious positions offered to a trauma surgeon at Manhattan Grace, only to find out that the only reason she was chosen to tour the country and work with Dr. Carroll was that her father was friends with Dr. Carroll. They played a few rounds of golf in the Hamptons. Even her brother-in-law pulled strings for her as if she couldn't make it on her own.

It just shook the foundation of everything Sarah had thought she knew.

It had knocked her confidence completely. Perhaps she wasn't the surgeon that she'd thought she was? So she'd turned down the position, much to her father's chagrin.

This was why she distanced herself from people. So many people trying to control the course of her life. She just couldn't trust anyone.

Not even herself.

Do you know how many strings I've had to pull for you over the years? Just so you can play doctor? Come to your senses, Sarah.

Sarah came to her senses all right. She threw the job back in her father's face, sold her apartment on the Upper West Side and took the job offer from Silas Draven to be the general practitioner and general surgeon at his newly opened ski lodge.

The ski lodge was set to open in one month, on Valentine's Day, and Sarah couldn't wait to get started. It would be a slower pace of life, but at least she would be able to help people here. She could be a doctor and not worry that her father was pulling strings to get her whatever she wanted. She was burned-out and really didn't know who she was or what she wanted anymore. She didn't even know if she wanted to be a surgeon and that thought terrified her, because for so long surgery had been her life.

For now a general practitioner sounded good. She could practice medicine and figure out where to go next. It sounded almost too good to be true.

Yeah. She could do this.

She smiled to herself and picked up her diploma from Stanford, in its frame, which was looking so forlorn on her desk. In fact her whole office was a complete disaster, with boxes and supplies scattered everywhere.

This was not an office yet. She couldn't see patients in a place that looked as if a storage unit had exploded. It wasn't very professional.

"Time to make this place my own." She spied the stepladder that had been left by the painters in the corner. She grabbed a hammer and a nail. She'd never hammered anything in her life, but there was always a first time for everything.

"I can do this," she said, as if trying to reassure herself. How hard could it be to hammer a nail into a wall? She had this. Except where she wanted to put the nail in was a little out of her reach for the stepladder. So she climbed to the very top of the ladder and held the wall for a bit of balance. Her perch was precarious, but all she was doing was hammering in one nail and it wasn't that big of a drop down to the carpet.

She lined up the nail and held the hammer, ready to drive the nail home.

"Did you check for a stud?" a male voice asked from behind.

"What...?" Sarah turned, surprised that someone had

snuck into her office and she hadn't heard them, but in the process of turning around she forgot what a precarious perch she had on the top of the stepladder and lost her footing.

Sarah closed her eyes and waited for her backside to hit the floor, but instead she found herself landing in two very strong arms and being held against a broad, muscular chest.

"You shouldn't stand on the top of a..." He trailed off.

"Who are you to tell me...?" Sarah opened her eyes and bit back a gasp as she stared up at the most stunningly handsome man she'd ever seen. Brown hair, with just a bit of curl, deep blue eyes and a neat beard, which just added to the ruggedness of his face.

Those blue eyes of his were wide with surprise and then she had the niggling sensation that she'd seen this face before, but couldn't recall when or where.

"What in the name of all that's good and holy were you doing up there with a hammer?" he demanded as he quickly set her down on her feet and took a step back from her as if she were on fire.

"Excuse me?" she asked. Who did this guy think he was?

"I'm telling you that wasn't a smart move climbing up on that ladder. You could've killed yourself if I hadn't showed up."

"Why did you show up? Who are you?"

His blue eyes flashed and he crossed his arms, fixing her with a stare that was meant to frighten her. Well, it didn't scare her.

"I'm here to take you out."

"Out? I don't believe I made any dates with anyone since I arrived in town."

He smirked. "Not on a date, darling. Though if I were to go on a date with someone, you're quite the fetching thing."

"Fetching? Darling?"

He held up his hands. "Look, I was teasing. I'm not interested in dating coworkers, let alone headstrong doctors from out east. I'm to take you out on the skis to show you some of the private residences being built and how to access them."

"Oh." She was slightly disappointed. Not that she had any interest in dating a mountain man, but a fling might've been fun. Especially since this mountain man was deliciously handsome.

Don't think like that. You're here to prove yourself, not date.

Sarah didn't date.

Her parents had tried over and over, setting her up with the *right* sort of man. Well, in their eyes anyway. It was just easier to concentrate on work and not bother with dating, romance or sex.

All the right kind of men Sarah had dated briefly in her early twenties were all wrong. It never felt right. There was never that spark or connection one was supposed to feel when falling in love with someone, but then again, since she'd never experienced it, maybe it was just a myth.

Men seemed to gravitate to her because she was a socialite and came from money. It was all about status for them, and as she was too focused on her career, she never pursued a man on her own and she never made the time to look for a man beyond her parents' circles.

Single life was so much easier.

And lonely.

"Do you know how to ski?" he asked disparagingly, breaking her chain of thoughts.

"No." Then she groaned inwardly at the thought of going back outside in the cold.

"I thought as much," he said condescendingly. "Well, I'll give you a few minutes to suit up so we can head out."

It was the tone that sparked a vivid memory for her suddenly. She could see those dark blue eyes glittering above a surgical mask. Defying her.

Get out of my OR!

Not on your life.

No way. It couldn't be him. It just couldn't be him.

"What's wrong?" he asked. "Don't like the cold?"

"It's not that. I think I know you."

He smiled. "Do you?"

"What's your name?" she asked.

Don't be him. Don't be him.

Then he grinned like the cat who'd got the cream. "Dr. Luke Ralston."

Damn, but then she was ticked. She'd put that memory of her time in Missoula far from her mind, not giving it much of a second thought because, really, what did it matter? She was in New York, let Luke Ralston have Montana.

Besides, Shane Draven had pulled through.

It was all trivial. Except now she was in Montana, working on their patient's uncle's resort and Dr. Luke Ralston was her coworker? This was a totally messed-up situation. Something she was not comfortable with.

"You knew exactly who I was."

Luke shrugged. "Not at first, but when you fell into my arms it all came back to me."

"And you didn't say anything? Like, maybe, 'Hey,

we know each other, we've worked together before' or something like that?"

He shrugged again and then hooked his thumbs into the belt loops on the waist of his tight, tight jeans. "What does it matter?"

"It matters a lot. You're a jerk!"

"Why am I a jerk? I mean, I did save you from probably concussing yourself or something."

"You were the guy I talked to in the hallway in Missoula. When I asked who Dr. Ralston was, you said you didn't know where he was. You lied to me."

"I didn't really want to argue with you in the hallway. I was on my way to the ICU to check on my patient. To make sure he pulled through surgery."

"He was my patient."

He grinned, smugly. "I brought him down off that mountain. He was my patient. You were just a locum surgeon. You didn't stay to make sure he made it through the night. You headed back east, to wherever you came from. I knew nothing about you and I didn't trust you. Of course, now you're going to be a regular here in town."

"Had I known there was a Ralston in Crater Lake I would've turned the job down."

Luke chuckled. "You must've taken this job on an impulse, then."

"Why do you say that?"

"If you'd researched Crater Lake you'd realize the family practice in town is run by a Ralston. I wasn't really hiding my identity. Not in my town."

Damn. He was right. She hadn't really looked to see what physicians were in town. She'd taken the job so quickly. She'd just been so eager to get out of New York City and away from her father's control. Crater Lake had sounded like a nice small town, and a job catering to the rich and famous in a resort had sounded perfect. It was a chance to prove herself to those who moved in her parents' circles.

Then maybe she could step out of her father's shadow. She wouldn't be Sarah Ledet, New York heiress and daughter of Vin Ledet, one of the wealthiest men on the eastern seaboard. She'd be Dr. Ledet, physician.

"You're regretting your decision to take this job, aren't you?" Luke asked. "I can see it on your face. You look absolutely horrified."

"Not the job, just who I have to work with."

He grinned and then laughed. "You're still a spitfire."

"Spitfire?"

"It's a compliment."

Sarah tried not to smile. She didn't want to smile. He was the jerk who'd disrupted her OR, given her a hard time and then lied to her. He was the one who'd questioned her surgical procedure and every move she'd made on that patient until she'd snapped. Only his smile had been infectious and she couldn't remember the last time she'd laughed, even though she was ticked off that it was him. The thorn in her side from last summer, standing right there in her office.

She should just throw him out. As she should have done from her OR.

When she glanced back up at him the lighthearted mood had changed. He looked annoyed and uncomfortable.

"What?" she asked.

"Nothing."

"Something changed. Just a moment ago you were complimenting me and joking. Now you look annoyed."

"I'm annoyed we're wasting the light standing around pointing fingers."

"Okay, you're right. I'm sorry."

"Well, I would gear up. I don't have all day to wait around for you." He walked out of her office leaving her standing there absolutely confused.

What had just happened?

Sarah wasn't sure, but she knew it would be best to keep her distance from Luke Ralston, though that was going to be tricky seeing how she was about to be dragged out on the mountain in the bitter cold with a man who was a little bit dangerous.

Not just a little bit dangerous.

A lot.

CHAPTER TWO

DAMN. IT HAD to be the spitfire.

Luke had forgotten all about her when he'd returned to Crater Lake after Shane Draven had pulled through. For a while he'd thought of that trauma surgeon he'd butted heads with in Missoula, but as he'd dealt with the last messy stages of his divorce, he'd put her from his mind.

Dealing with his ex just reminded him of all the reasons why he didn't trust women or romantic entanglements.

It hurt too much, but Christine wasn't the only reason. Hurt went both ways. He liked his life too much and part of that was doing risky things to save lives up on the mountain.

He'd given up his life in the army for a woman he loved and look how that turned out.

To live the life he'd made for himself since leaving the army, he couldn't have love. He wouldn't give up his life for anyone.

He threw himself completely into his work and avoided hanging around the town of Crater Lake as much as possible. It was bad enough being divorced, but having your ex-wife and former best friend, who was now your ex's husband, living and working in the town you grew up in was a little too much for him.

The problem was, his former best friend was the town sheriff. That was why they were staying in Crater Lake, but Luke wouldn't be driven out of town.

He'd grown up here. He was going to stay here.

And an injury to his leg during an avalanche last winter prevented him from returning to active duty, even after giving up his commission.

Besides, he preferred being up on the mountain.

He liked being alone in his cabin. He liked the work; though he missed surgery and envied Carson just a bit for seeing patients every day, there was no way he could've chained himself to a desk, to an office or a hospital. He would suffocate, but he'd been willing to do it for Christine.

Maybe if you hadn't joined the army Christine wouldn't have left. Maybe you could've been happy.

Only his call of duty had been strong. He'd always wanted to serve and further his medical education in the army. And Christine had known that when they'd got together.

Luke cursed under his breath.

No, she would've left. Just as he hadn't wanted to change the course of his career, Christine hadn't wanted to be his wife. Of course now he wasn't a soldier, but by the time his career in the army was over Christine was over him.

No, he wasn't going to think about her. She'd broken his heart and he wouldn't let her or anyone else make him feel that way again.

Why did it have to be her? Why did it have to be the spitfire?

Silas hadn't told him the name of the physician who would be working at the resort. All he'd said was that she was from out east and had asked if Luke could train her on mountain survival and survival medicine.

She's from money, Ralston. I'm sure she's been on skis, but probably not in a way that would satisfy your sensibilities.

Which was why Luke was here. It was just fate was a bit sick and twisted by making that physician Dr. Ledet, the surgeon he'd butted heads with.

As if dealing with her in the summer wasn't enough? Maybe it was karma? He'd teased Carson when Esme Petersen had come to town. Perhaps this was retribution?

The only difference was Carson had found love with Esme and Luke was not looking for that at all.

Carson hadn't been looking, either.

"Is this okay?"

Luke shook that little voice from his head and glanced over at Sarah. She had a good parka on, waterproof mitts, a hat with ear flaps, boots, but nothing on her legs except black stretchy pants that fit her curves like a glove. His blood heated.

Think about something else.

"Where are your snow pants?" Luke asked, tearing his gaze away from her. He didn't want to look at her at the moment. He had to regain control.

"Snow pants?"

"Don't you ski?"

"I told you before, no. I've never skied."

"Doesn't every eastern WASP rich girl ski? Isn't that what the Poconos are for?"

Her stare was icy cold and she put her hands on those

curvy hips. Hips he'd thought about touching himself. "Excuse me?"

Luke groaned. He wasn't going to get in an argument with her. "You need snow pants. If you fall out there and your pants get wet there's no way we're turning around so you can change. I'm here to teach you survival skills. If you were out there on your own, there would be no option to change. You'd freeze to death."

Sarah still looked as if she were going to skewer him alive. "Fine. I'll find some snow pants, but, really, stereotyping me, that was so not cool."

"If the shoe fits."

She cocked her eyebrows and smirked. "Oh, really? Didn't we have this argument in the summer? I seem to recall bits and pieces of it..."

He groaned. "Fine. You're right. I did accuse you of stereotyping me. I apologize, but, really, put on some snow pants before we lose the light."

"Fine and, for your information, not all of us 'rich girls' ski. Some of us prefer yachts and sailing." She winked and then disappeared into her office again.

Luke rolled his eyes, but couldn't help but laugh to himself. He still admired her spunk.

When she came out of her office again, she was properly attired.

"Good, now let's get down to the ski shack and get geared up. I'm going to take you up the first of the four main trails at this resort."

Sarah fell into step behind him; the only sound was the swishing of the nylon fabric rubbing together as they walked down the hall and outside. Luke tried not to laugh, because just under that sound was some muttering. And maybe some bad words, but he couldn't quite tell.

"I feel like a marshmallow," she mumbled. "Do I look like one?"

"Yes. You do, but it will keep you warm." He helped open the door to outside. "Ms. Marshmallow."

With a huff Sarah pushed past him out into the snow. "You're a bit of a jerk. Has anyone ever told you that?"

"Several people."

There was a twinkle to her eye and she smiled slightly. "Good."

"Well, now that's all settled. Let's get the skis on and head out." He led the way to the ski shack, which was closed up. It would open on more regular hours when the resort had its official grand opening on Valentine's Day. Right now, Luke had full run of it and of all the equipment.

It was one of the perks he liked about working for Silas Draven. He wasn't a huge fan of skiing, but cross-country skiing on the mountain trails was the only way to access some of the remote residents of Crater Lake. His horse just couldn't handle the deep snow that collected on the side of the mountain in the winter.

And he would never put his horse in the way of a possible avalanche.

He glanced over to the southern peak, to the forest that was thick, before it disappeared into the alpine zone of the mountain. Old Nestor lived up in that dense forest.

Nestor was a hermit. He liked to live off the grid and away from everyone else. Luke admired him and went to check on him often. Nestor was the one who'd taught him many things about surviving on the mountain, since Nestor had been living up on the mountain for as long as Luke could remember and before that.

Only, Nestor was getting old and in the winter the cold

bothered him something fierce. So Luke was thankful for access to skis and snowshoes. It made checking on Nestor that much easier.

He unlocked the door and headed over to the rack.

"Oh, cool! Snowshoes," Sarah remarked. "I've always wanted to try them."

"Really?" he asked, surprised.

She nodded. "Anything to make walking on snow easier."

"Snowshoeing is just as much work as skiing. Skis can move you faster."

"Yeah, but cross-country skis don't go uphill. You said you wanted me to learn how to access trails and stuff. Shouldn't I be snowshoeing?"

She's got a point. Skiing will only get you so far.

"You're right," Luke admitted. "Okay. We'll add snowshoes to our pack."

"Pack?"

Luke picked up the large rucksack that he'd stuffed full of emergency and survival gear. The pack was probably half the size of Sarah and when he held it up to her, her eyes widened and her mouth opened for a moment in surprise.

Then she shrugged. "Sure. That's reasonable. Just out of curiosity, though, what's in it?"

"Don't you know?"

She glared at him. "Really?"

"You should know."

"I don't. I've never lived near a mountain. I'm from Manhattan."

Luke shook his head. "Hey, I was trying not to stereotype you."

"I ought to slug you."

He laughed at that. He couldn't help himself; it was easy to tease her. He was enjoying the banter. "I'm sorry. I'll stop."

She crossed her arms. "Fine or I could start talking about mountain men."

"What do you know about mountain men?" he asked.

Sarah shook her head. "Tell me what's in the bag."

Luke knelt down and unzipped it. "This is a standard pack to help you survive in a winter climate on the mountain."

"So I'll only need to carry around this stuff in the winter?"

"No," Luke said. "Some things can be left behind, but if you're working up near the Alpine zone or higher, you'd be surprised how cold it can get even in the heat of summer."

"Okay, so always be prepared for snow?"

He nodded. "Yep. So in this pack you have your essentials like first-aid kit. The only thing I haven't packed in here is a change of clothes for you so I just packed some of my old clothes. If worse comes to worst you can always wear those."

Her cheeks reddened slightly, as if she was blushing, but Luke could've been wrong. It could've been the wind.

She cleared her throat. "Go on."

"Canteen for water."

"What about melting snow?"

Luke cocked an eyebrow. "You're going to need something to carry it in. I also have a pot, ice pick, rope, matches, GPS, topographical map of the area, one day's worth of rations, sleeping bag and an axe."

"It's like you're camping."

"If you get lost out there, yeah, you'll be 'camping'

until help arrives." Then he held out something he was sure she'd never seen before. "This is one of the most important things."

"A compass?"

"Close. It's an altimeter."

"A what?" she asked.

"It's a barometric altimeter. It measures changes in atmosphere. The higher you go, the lower the pressure is. If your GPS or compass isn't working, this can be used along with the map to determine where you are. I'll show you how to use it."

"Good, because seriously my eyes were glazing over there for a second." She laughed nervously and he handed her the altimeter to look at. "Though, really, won't you know if you're at the top of the mountain? How can you get lost if you're up there?"

"You can get lost all right and if you're not used to high altitude you can get acute mountain sickness. Dr. Petersen in town suffered from it last year. Just ask her."

"Dr. Petersen? There's a female doctor in town? I thought the other doctor was your brother."

"Dr. Petersen is a cardio surgeon. She's opened a clinic in partnership with my brother. She sees a lot of heart patients from around this area."

"Huh, I wonder what would make a cardio-thoracic surgeon settle down in a place like this," Sarah wondered out loud. "I mean, the nearest hospital is quite a bit away."

"Why did you?" Luke asked.

The question caught her off guard, because she blushed again and quickly started examining the altimeter.

Did it really matter?

It shouldn't matter to him, but he couldn't help but

wonder why. There weren't many single people in Crater Lake. It was small. When they'd first got together, Christine had wanted to stay in Crater Lake, and when he got his posting to Germany she wouldn't go with him. She didn't want to live on a base. She didn't want to be an army wife. So she'd decided to stay and start a family with Anthony.

A family he wanted so desperately.

A family he was never going to have.

Don't think about it.

"Come on, I'll pack the snowshoes, as well. We have some distance to travel and some more stuff I have to show you before it gets too dark, and it gets dark here early." He took the altimeter back from her and packed it in the knapsack.

He didn't have time to focus on the past. To focus on his past hurts or the things he would never have.

He was here to do a job and that was to show Dr. Sarah Ledet how to survive on the mountain. That was all. Once he'd done that, he never had to see her again and he was going to make sure that happened.

Sarah thought her lungs were going to burst. She was sweaty and exhausted. Parts of her that she hadn't even known existed ached and each breath was harder to take.

At least I'm not cold.

She just shook her head and leaned up against a tree as Luke set their skis against a fence line that ran on one side of the trail. He glanced over at her.

"You okay? You look tired."

Of course I'm tired, but she wasn't going to tell him that. All her life she'd been labelled and she'd had enough of it.

"I'm fine. Just catching my breath."

He frowned. "If you get a headache or feel ill, let me know right away. That's a sign of mountain sickness."

"Will do." She didn't feel sick and didn't have a headache. All she was was sweaty and tired. "You said Dr. Petersen had this? How did she get over it?"

"You get off the mountain."

"I live on the mountain."

Luke chuckled. "You don't live that far up the mountain, though."

"I thought it was pretty high up, considering I used to live pretty close to sea level."

"Never thought about it that way." Luke pulled out the snowshoes that had been strapped to the back of the enormous pack Sarah had had on her back, which was now resting under a fir tree on a bed of needles so as not to get wet.

Maybe she was picking up mountain survival a bit.

"You ready for snowshoeing?"

Sarah groaned. "How about we head for home? I'm sure it will be faster downhill on our skis."

Luke chuckled. "We'll head down soon enough. I want to see you practice on these. Just up the trail the snow gets pretty deep. Too deep for skis."

"No one lives up that trail."

"Right, not now, but when this trail is groomed regularly and a lone cross-country skier or snowshoer gets injured or lost up there, you're going to have to know how to get to them."

Sarah sighed, but then took the snowshoes and strapped them on. They were quite easy and didn't look like she'd expected them to. They were made of aluminum and nylon.

"Take a step and tell me what you think," he said as he moved back and then clamped his on.

Sarah began to walk up the trail and it took her a few times to really find her stride, but it wasn't all that bad.

"I think this is easier than the skiing, to be honest." She bounced in her step. "I could get used to these."

"Just be careful," Luke called out over his shoulder.

"Of wha…?" She spoke too soon as she lost her footing and toppled face-first into a large snowdrift. Snow shot up her nose and into her mouth, burning.

I hate winter. I hate winter.

"Are you okay?" Luke was beside her and she could hear the amusement in his voice.

"Fine," she said as she wiped her face. "I really wasn't expecting to do a face-plant with snowshoes on. Skis for sure, but snowshoes. I know I'm klutzy."

"Well, at least this time I didn't have to catch you." He rubbed some of the snow from her face and a rush of butterflies invaded her stomach as she looked up into his eyes. He was smiling at her, but it was tender, as if he really cared that she'd done a horrible face-plant in the snow.

Of course the butterflies could be from that mountain sickness, but somehow she didn't think so.

"Thanks," she said, looking away and glad the snow had made her cheeks red, because if it hadn't he would surely see her blush.

"You should've been wearing your goggles to protect your eyes. Goggles don't belong on your forehead."

"I forgot to put them back on after my break. I was wearing them when we were skiing."

Luke helped her to her feet, his strong arms around

her waist as he righted her. She liked the feeling of his arms around her, steadying her. It was comforting.

You don't date. You can't date.

Her mother would set her up on the occasional date, but those were all with men who would take care of her. Who just wanted her to be this pretty, well-dressed society wife. None of them were really interested in her and she'd been burned too many times.

And she never had time to find men on her own, because she was working so darn hard to show her parents that she could have it all, that she didn't need a man to take care of her. That she was old enough to take care of herself.

Men were off-limits.

Of course, her father admitting that he'd had a hand in almost every aspect of her career made her think that all that hard work, all those hours she'd put in weren't worth it. Maybe she should've been out there partying, being seen in all the right places with all the right people, just like her older sister.

Really?

She shook her head. That was all in the past, though. She was in Crater Lake now. In a job of her own choosing and she planned to make the most of it. Even if it meant traipsing around in the snow with the sexiest mountain man she'd ever laid eyes on.

A man that also drove her a bit crazy.

"You ready to try again?" Luke asked.

"Sure. The sooner we get this done, the sooner I can head back to my apartment in the resort and curl up in front of a fire."

"Glad to see you're on board." Luke went over and picked up the knapsack. "You're going to need this."

Sarah moaned as it was placed over her shoulders again. "Thanks. I almost forgot."

"It's your lifeline up here. You can't forget. We'll do a half-mile hike up this trail through the snow, we'll triage a fake patient I have up there and then head back down to the resort. That's after we build a makeshift stretcher."

"You have a patient up there?" Sarah asked. "Who in their right mind would wait out in the cold for hours for you?"

Luke winked. "It's a dummy."

"Clearly."

He rolled his eyes. "It's a simulation. A mannequin. It's not a real person, but it's simulating a very real situation."

Sarah sighed. "Okay. Lead on."

Luke nodded and pulled on his own pack. She watched him for a few moments as he broke a path ahead of her. Even though he was wearing thick snow pants you could still make out the outline of his strong, muscular thighs and his tight butt.

Sarah shook her head. It was apparent she was suffering from altitude sickness, because she was thinking about the strangest things.

Dr. Luke Ralston was off-limits.

He worked for Silas Draven as well, so that meant it was a no go for her. She didn't mix business with pleasure.

So she couldn't think about Luke that way.

She just couldn't.

CHAPTER THREE

It had been three days since she last saw Dr. Luke Ralston and that was a good thing after the torment he'd put her through up on that high mountain trail. He hadn't been kidding about a simulation. When they'd got to the mannequin, it had been half-buried in ice and under a tree trunk. There had been broken skis and fake blood.

Sarah had never picked up an axe before, but she did that day. She had the blister and the splinters to prove it.

Even though she'd wanted to tell Luke his simulation was cracked, she hadn't backed down. She knew that he thought of her as some kind of spoiled rich girl and that was far from the truth. So she'd learned quite quickly how to use an axe. She'd shown him a thing or two.

She'd also learned how to make a makeshift gurney out of broken skis, rope, a tarp and duct tape. After assessing the mannequin's ABCs, they'd got him on their gurney and down off the mountain.

There had been quite a few stares as she'd come down to the lodge with a mannequin on a stretcher splattered with craft-store paint. Still, she'd done it and he'd grudgingly admitted that she'd done a good job and that was the last she'd seen of him.

She thought she was going to be put through some

more training, but so far she hadn't seen him. She should be happy about that and she was, but she wasn't totally. She looked for him everywhere, as if he were going to pop out of the shadows and frighten her. The thought of seeing him actually made her excited, as if she were some young girl with a crush.

There was no denying Luke was handsome. She'd thought that the first moment she saw him. But there was something else about him. A lone wolf quality. He was a man who didn't want or need anyone else. The kind of man who was completely untamed.

He was a challenge, and she'd always liked a challenge.

Focus.

She couldn't think about him that way. Distance. That was what she needed. Right now this time was about her. Career was her life.

If she got together with someone, her parents would never believe she could function on her own. That she was a surgeon.

Even then, she wasn't sure of anything. Everything she'd thought she earned had really come because she was Vin Ledet's daughter. Her father knew people on the admissions board at college. She'd fought so hard for her MCAT scores, achieving one of the highest that year, which should've been enough to get her into medical school, but apparently not enough for her father. Then her residency and her fellowship, her father had had a hand in that. Everything she'd pursued in her medical career her father had had a hand in.

No wonder her belief in herself was fleeting.

Except this place.

She'd earned this on her own by saving Silas Draven's nephew Shane in Missoula.

Silas and her father moved in the same circles and never saw eye to eye.

Sarah knew it wasn't because of who her father was. This job was because of her own merit.

Someone believed in her abilities and she wasn't going to let them down.

She could do this.

This was her focus and she was going to prove to everyone she was up to the task. This clinic was going to be her pride and joy.

Her clinic had opened a bit earlier than she'd planned, but Silas Draven had had a large party of tourists coming in and he'd wanted to make sure that it was up and running. He wanted his resort to be all-inclusive, and didn't want his guests having to go into town and wait at the local clinic.

Even though the resort hadn't officially opened, the large party of skiers was certainly giving her a run for her money. Her clinic had been full the two days she'd been open. It was usually just minor stuff, cuts and sunburns, but she was enjoying the work and, the best part, it was honest work. Though, she missed surgery, the rush of the hospital, but this job she'd got on her own.

Her parents didn't have a hand in it.

Really, Sarah? Sunburns? The only sun you should think about is evening out your tan.

She cursed under her breath, trying to shake away her sister's annoying voice. Her sister had never said those exact words, but she could almost picture her, standing in the waiting room and saying them, because her sister had nagged her about similar things before.

"Patient ten?" Sarah briefly looked up from her chart, to the busy waiting room at her clinic. "Patient number ten?"

A man with a very red face stood up and walked toward her. He nodded and winced. "I am Mr. Fontblanc."

Sarah smiled. "I know, we just use a numbering system here to keep anonymity."

"Ah, oui. Merci beaucoup."

"You can have a seat in exam room one. I'll be with you momentarily."

Mr. Fontblanc nodded again, shuffling off down the hall. She looked at her chart one more time and was about to call the next victim of a really bad sunburn when the door to her clinic burst open. Luke strode into her pristine clinic, dirty and breathless.

"What're you doing?" he asked.

"I'm seeing patients," Sarah said, trying not to look at him. Distance was the key.

"Good, I have a patient for you."

"What? Where?"

"He's in the lobby."

"In the lobby? Why is he in the lobby?"

Luke rolled his eyes and crossed his arms. "Would you stop giving me the third degree and just come to the lobby?"

"I have a patient waiting in my exam room. I can't leave him there."

"Is your patient bleeding profusely with a head injury?"

"That's confidential."

Luke shook his head and pushed past her into the exam room.

"Dr. Ralston!" Sarah tried to stop him, but he was in the exam room. Mr. Fontblanc looked a bit stunned.

"Sorry to keep you waiting..." Luke peered at the man. "Too much sun?"

"*Oui*...uh, yes."

"Vous êtes Français?" Luke inquired in perfect French.

"Oui."

Sarah stood back, stunned. She didn't know French at all. Spanish, she knew quite a bit, but French, she was at a loss. Luke seemed to know it. He questioned the man briefly and then pulled out a tube of topical cream from her medicine cupboard, handing it to her patient and then patting him on the back.

The patient still seemed shell-shocked, but overall was happy.

"Merci."

"Pas de problème," Luke said.

The patient left the room and Luke turned back to her. "You ready to go and help the patient in the lobby now?"

"What just happened here?" She watched as Luke began to grab suturing trays, gauze and a bolus for an IV. "What's going on? Why are you stealing my supplies?"

He groaned and grabbed her hand. "Come on. I need another doctor's help with this."

Sarah didn't really have much of a choice as she was dragged from her clinic. The other patients watched her leave, just as confused as she was at the moment.

"If this patient needs another doctor, why didn't you get your brother to help you?" Sarah asked.

"There was no time to take this man to town." Luke pushed the button on the elevator, not looking at her, but watching for the door to light up and open.

"What's wrong with the patient?" she asked.

"Have you ever seen a mauling?"

Sarah gasped. "Did you just say a mauling? By what?"

Luke glanced at her. "A bear."

She shook her head. She'd seen pictures in textbooks when she was a resident. As a trauma surgeon you had to be prepared for everything, but she'd never actually encountered one personally. She was aware of the damage that could be done. Her stomach twisted in a knot at the very idea, but they were in bear country. It was to be expected.

The elevator arrived and they got on. It was a quick ride down to the lobby. When the doors opened everything was in chaos and Sarah could see a trail of blood from the door to a boardroom down a darkened hall.

"I don't get it," Sarah remarked as she fell into step beside Luke.

"What don't you get?" he asked.

"Bears hibernate. It's January."

Luke sighed. "No, not really. It's called torpor. It's like hibernation—they can be woken. This idiot was fool enough to stumble on a bear's den and, instead of leaving the bear well enough alone, he crawled inside to get a picture. Thankfully, people were with him."

"Idiot is right."

He nodded. "If you haven't seen a mauling before, prepare yourself."

She nodded. "I've seen worse stuff in the ER."

"Possible disembowelment and bite marks?"

"Yeah. A car can do damage to a patient, too. I'm ready."

A small smile played on his lips, but just briefly. It was almost as if he was impressed that she didn't shy away or that she wasn't squeamish at the prospect. It scared her. It was something she was completely unfamiliar with. It was something she was a little terrified about herself since moving from Manhattan to a remote town in northwest Montana, but this was her job. She was going to help Luke any way that she could. It was the trauma surgeon in her.

"Did you bring enough supplies down?" she asked.

"We've got enough supplies in here. We have to get him stabilized before the air ambulance gets here."

Sarah nodded. "Okay."

She walked into the room and tried not to gasp. The man was in bad shape. There were deep lacerations to his arm, his legs and torso, but his face was really bad. She could see teeth marks, deep gouging all over; she could see bone on his arm and the bandages on his abdomen were already soaked through, which tipped Sarah off that this guy would need packing if he was going to survive the trip to the nearest hospital. The way his abdomen was distended, she knew from her trained eye he would suffer from compartment syndrome sooner rather than later and that could be fatal if not controlled.

"Buddy, I've brought another doctor here to help me." Luke spoke to the man. "Just take it easy."

The man just moaned.

"I'm surprised he's lucid."

"Me, too," Luke said. "I did give him a shot of morphine in the field when I found him, but he's lost a lot of blood."

Sarah nodded and pulled off her white lab coat. "Gloves?"

Luke gestured in the direction of the sideboard, where a box of rubber gloves was waiting. She slipped on a pair and then grabbed a pack of gauze.

"I need you to hold him down—I'm going to put in a central line," Luke told her.

"You're going to put in a central line here?"

He nodded. "No choice. Look at his arms, and his veins are chunky. The bear did damage. Lots of damage."

"Sure." Sarah leaned over and held the man down. She looked down into his dark eyes, full of confusion and fear. "Don't worry, sir. We're going to get you patched up in no time. Soon you won't be in so much pain. I promise."

"Hold him now for me," Luke said.

"I've got him. Just do it."

Luke inserted the central line quickly and efficiently. She couldn't remember the last time she'd seen someone put in a central line so fast before. She was impressed. The patient barely flinched, but that could be because maybe some of the fight had gone out of him, or it could've been the morphine.

Once he was hooked up to a drip, he passed out and Luke went about stitching what they could to help control the bleeding. Sarah packed his face and set a broken bone in his arm. They didn't say much to each other; there wasn't much to say, really. They were both totally focused on their patient.

The last time they'd worked on a patient together, they were at each other's throats. This was different. It was nice. Comforting almost, as if she'd been doing this with him for a long, long time, and she couldn't remember the last time she'd felt such a familiarity with another surgeon before.

"He has extensive damage to his abdomen. There is nothing I can do here."

"Pack him?" Luke asked.

She nodded. "No choice. If I start poking around to find the source of the bleeders I could do more damage. His body needs to rest before repairs. Does bear saliva have an envenomation? You know, like the wolverine or Komodo dragon?"

"No, but the saliva often carries staph or strep, which can lead to infections and organ shutdown." He frowned and seemed upset for a brief moment. "Either way he'll need a good course of antibiotics, tetanus and rabies. Though rabies from bear bites are rare."

"Why is that?"

"The injury rate from bear attacks in North America is like one person per couple million. Of course, that report by S. Herrero is from 1970. It could be different now."

"Wow."

"The more we encroach on their territory, the worse it gets. I read a lot on animal attacks for obvious reasons."

"Makes sense."

She would have never thought about reading medical papers on animal attacks before coming here. It wasn't something that happened a lot in Manhattan. She'd dealt with dog, cat and human bites in the city.

It was time to broaden her reading if she was going to stay here.

Luke impressed her with his knowledge and that was a hard thing to do. She liked working with him. They could work on the patient seamlessly and still chat easily. She'd never had that kind of rapport with another surgeon before.

It felt so right working with him. It was just sad that this poor man had to suffer and Sarah decided right then and there: she didn't want to mess with a bear in any way, shape or form.

When they had done all they could do, they just monitored him and waited for the air ambulance to come. Nothing but the sound of the portable monitors between them.

"How long do you think it will be before the air ambulance comes?" Sarah asked, breaking the silence.

"Should be here soon, though there was a storm rolling in from the southwest. I hope that didn't hinder the flight in from Missoula."

"If it does?" she asked.

"Great Falls will send one. Missoula is bigger, though."

She nodded and there was a knock at the door. A paramedic stood there. "Someone call an air ambulance?"

They worked with the paramedics to get the patient onto the stretcher and then out into the cold to the waiting ambulance, which would take him down to the airport. The ambulance had landed on Silas Draven's private airstrip.

Once the patient was loaded up the ambulance flicked on its sirens and headed down the long windy road to Crater Lake. Sarah didn't stand outside for too long because it was cold and she didn't have her coat on.

Luke followed her back inside.

"I hope he makes it," Sarah remarked.

"He will. Death is rare. Although compartment syndrome worries me."

"Me, too," Sarah said. "Glad you caught that, as well."

"I've seen compartment syndrome many a time as an army medic. The bowels inflating, then the liver and kidneys begin to shut down. It's a domino effect."

"It is. I thought you would've followed him. Didn't

you get him down off the mountain?" she teased, as that had been the reason why he'd stood in her OR last summer questioning her every move.

"I usually would, but he woke a bear up. The bear just didn't go back to sleep. I have to track it and…" He trailed off.

"What?"

"I have to make sure it goes back to its den, but, since the bear has been fully woken up from its torpor, it's going to be looking for food. I don't want to have to destroy it."

She frowned. "Oh. I hope you don't have to do that."

"Me, too. It's not the bear's fault that moron decided it would be a good selfie. Me with a bear."

Sarah chuckled. "A tourist?"

"Close, a surveyor. A new one. The surveyors I train to work up in these mountains know better than that."

"I'm sure they do, but I didn't see his pack."

Luke chuckled. "I think he left it up there on the mountain."

"How are his friends?"

"Shaken up. I should go talk to them."

"Do you want me to?"

"No. It's okay. I can. Thanks for helping me," he said.

"I really didn't have a choice." She smiled at him.

"I'm sorry about that. I overstep my boundaries in emergency situations."

"It's no problem. That's what I'm here for. To help patients."

And then it hit her.

Oh. No.

"Darn it," she cursed out loud. "Darn it."

"What?" he asked.

"My patients in the clinic. How long was I gone for?"

Luke glanced at his wrist. "About forty minutes."

Sarah groaned. "If they complain to Mr. Draven..."

"If they complain I will tell him you helped one of his employees who was dumb enough to stick his face in a bear's den."

"I think Mr. Draven will be more ticked about the patients in my clinic, though."

Luke frowned. "Come on. We'll tell them why."

"Are you serious? We have to protect privacy rights."

"They won't know him. These are tourists. Tourists like bear stories."

Sarah looked at him as if he were crazy. Maybe he was. Maybe he'd spent too many winters up on that mountain and he'd lost his mind. Her patients were going to be mad that she'd left them up there for that long.

Mr. Draven had made it pretty clear that he wanted patients to be seen within twenty minutes of their arrival and registration at the clinic. Not forty.

"I don't know. I don't think that's a good idea."

Luke rolled his eyes and then took her hand. It shocked her. It was calloused, warm and strong. It sent a tingle of electricity through her and she could feel the heat flooding her cheeks at just the simple act of a touch from him, but then she wasn't used to physical intimacy. It had been so long and her parents weren't exactly huggers. So that simple touch threw her for a loop.

"Come on, we don't have to tell the particulars, but you can bet when I warn that group of European tourists off the mountain trails because of a bear being at large, that will get them talking."

"Or send them packing." Sarah grudgingly let him lead her back to her clinic. "If it were me and I heard that about a bear, I would be packing my bags and leaving the general vicinity. Bears are beautiful animals, but I never want to encounter one in the wild."

He shook his head. "That's because you haven't been properly trained on how to deal with a bear in the wild."

"Please don't show me."

He laughed and pushed the button to the elevator, the doors opening instantly. "If you're living in bear country, Sarah, you really don't have a choice in the matter. Everyone in Crater Lake needs to know what to do in case of a bear. Do you have bear deterrent?"

Sarah shook her head and pinched the bridge of her nose. "Oh, God."

"I take it you don't."

Sarah glanced up at him and could see he was enjoying her torment. "I have a spray can of something in my office, but I didn't buy it. It was just there when I took over."

"I know. I bought it and put it there. Most offices of the permanent staff have a can. It's better to be prepared and, since most of you aren't from Montana, I thought it would be the best."

"You're really enjoying this, aren't you?"

"Enjoying what?" A small smile played across his lips. It was a devious smile, even if it was partially hidden behind his beard. It was the kind that made her a bit weak in the knees and she fought the urge to kiss him. Even though she couldn't remember the last time she'd kissed a man. She resisted the urge to kiss him and gave him a playful shove instead.

"Hey, what was that for?"

"For enjoying my torment and for teasing me." Sarah shook her head. "What am I going to say?"

"Sorry would be a start."

"Not to you. The patients."

"I'll handle it. Besides you don't speak French."

She chuckled. "This is true."

The elevator dinged open and her stomach knotted. She hoped word wouldn't get back to Silas Draven that she'd left a big group of VIP tourists by themselves. She didn't need him to think she couldn't handle her job and she definitely didn't want this to get back to her father.

"Don't be nervous. It will be fine." Luke took her hand and she tried not to gasp at his familiarity. "Come on, you have to face the music."

She took her hand back and marched ahead of him, trying to put some distance between them. "Okay, we can do this."

Facing all those tourists was better than having him touch her. Not exactly better, but safer. Actually she'd rather face a bear over being alone with Luke. Luke was dangerous. He was the kind of dangerous she secretly yearned for. It was electric, intense and was, oh, so wrong.

The patients left in the waiting room were pacing and looked none too pleased when she walked in.

"I'm sorry," she began, but as the words came out the din of French was overwhelming.

Luke stepped into the fray and shouted over the noise. A few choice words and the noise ebbed and the patients sat down again.

"Do you have enough exam rooms for five people?" Luke asked out of the corner of his mouth.

"No, I have two."

Luke made a face. "I guess Mr. Draven didn't really think you'd be this busy on any given day."

"Or maybe he thought two would be enough. I'm sure he didn't expect me to be called away for a mauling."

"I'd call your next patient. I'll help you. We'll get them in and out fast.

"Really? You're going to help me."

"Of course."

Sarah nodded and picked up the discarded patient charts, handing Luke three and keeping two for herself.

"Hey, how come I get the majority?"

"You speak the language." She winked at him and then walked away. Pleased that she was tormenting him just as much as he was her, but most importantly she had to put distance between them.

"Patient eleven?" she called out.

Luke put the last of the files on Sarah's desk. She was typing away on her computer and didn't even bother to look up at him.

"There. All done. Two more sunburns. The French have mountains, don't they? Surely they ski."

"These guests are from an island in the Caribbean called Marie-Galante. It's tropical."

"That doesn't explain sunburns. They should know how to use sunblock."

"Snow sunburns. One of them told me they'd never seen snow before—they didn't think they could get a sunburn in the winter. Actually, I'm glad they spoke French and not Creole."

Luke grinned. "Me, too. I knew a Cajun man once in my unit."

"Right, you were a medic in the army."

"Yeah. Right." Luke should leave, the conversation was turning in a direction he wasn't comfortable with, but he couldn't pry himself away from her and he didn't know why. He was drawn to her. This was why he'd gone out into the woods for a few days.

He'd had to get out of temptation's way.

"Thanks again for helping me," she said. "It's been a while since I've been in a clinic."

"No problem. You helped me with the mauling, but honestly I'm surprised you're in a clinic. I thought you were a surgeon."

"I am a surgeon."

"So why did you leave the OR?"

Sarah's lips pursed together and he was wondering if maybe now he was making her uncomfortable, just as he'd felt moments ago when he'd unthinkingly mentioned his time in the army. Something he was not ready to talk about, because he did miss it and it reminded him of his failed marriage, which was something he wanted to forget.

So what had made Sarah leave surgery?

None of your business.

Only he couldn't help himself. She'd been such a bulldog in the OR last summer. Surgeons with that kind of drive and passion didn't just walk away.

You did.

"I wanted a change of pace," she said.

"A change of pace?"

She shrugged. "Sure, why not? The city was getting to me."

"Somehow I don't believe that."

"You want to talk about truths? Why did you leave the army?"

Luke's spine stiffened. "My tour of duty ended. Well, I better go. Thanks again."

"You're welcome."

He left her office, without so much as a look back. It was for the best. If he looked back, he might stay. The way that she'd looked at him, he knew that she didn't believe him. Heck, he wasn't even sure if he had convinced himself of that fact. This was why Sarah was dangerous. She affected him like no one else had. Not even Christine. Sarah got under his skin. She actually made him yearn for things he used to want. Things that he'd thought were long gone.

He didn't need that.

He didn't want that.

Didn't he?

CHAPTER FOUR

"SHE DID WHAT?"

"She signed out a pair of snowshoes and headed up the lake trail," said the equipment-rental guy. He looked a bit scared, which was good. Luke wanted to strike fear into the guy's heart. Didn't they know there was a bear loose? A bear that had mauled a guy two days ago. A bear that hadn't been tracked down yet.

What was she thinking? Clearly she wasn't. He had to find her before the bear did.

"What trail did she take?"

"The Lakeview trail."

"When did she leave?"

The rental guy looked confused and shrugged. "Like twenty minutes ago?"

"Why did you let her go out?"

The young man just stuttered. "I didn't know I wasn't supposed to. Besides, I just started my shift. She was heading out just as I came in."

Luke cursed under his breath. "Don't let anyone else out. There's a bear on the loose."

"Aren't bears supposed to be hibernating?"

Luke just shook his head and walked away from the

rental guy. He couldn't believe she'd gone out there. Why would she head out on her own?

You haven't seen her for a couple days. Maybe she thinks the bear has gone by now.

It was a foolish assumption. Anyone from around here would know to wait for the all-clear, or at least find out the areas the bear had been seen in.

She's not from around here. It was his fault. He should have explained it to her. Instead he'd kept his distance.

He'd avoided her because she was getting too close for him. Since he'd come home expecting to start a life with his wife and realized his life wasn't going to be how he'd pictured it, he'd been keeping people at a distance.

Less chance of getting hurt that way.

Except, he enjoyed being around Sarah. The back and forth with her was refreshing and it totally caught him off guard. He couldn't be around her, yet here he was, worried about her.

She most likely would be fine on the Lakeview trail as the bear's den was nowhere near that, but, still, she didn't know anything about the mountains.

Luke returned to the rental chalet. "Give me a pair of snowshoes, please."

Once he had the snowshoes secured to his knapsack, he climbed on his snowmobile and headed up to the Lakeview trail. When he got to the edge of the trail, he parked his snowmobile, strapped on his snowshoes, pulled on his rucksack and unstrapped the tranquilizer gun.

He could see Sarah's fresh tracks in the snow. She couldn't be too far off. He'd taken her out once; she was good, but she wasn't that good. He was confident that he could catch up with her in no time.

As he headed up the path, he soon saw her. She had stopped not that far into the trail, at a lookout. She was holding her camera and was taking pictures.

Luke watched her for a few moments. She had a really fancy camera. He didn't know much about cameras, but it looked high-tech. Sarah was completely immersed in what she was doing. She was very unaware of everything around her.

Her cheeks were flushed from the cold and the exercise, but she was smiling as she held up her camera and then he couldn't help but smile, too, watching her. It was enchanting.

She's so beautiful.

And he shook his head, because he couldn't think about her like that. She was off-limits to him. It was a beautiful vista; he couldn't really blame her for that. Crater Lake was a beautiful place. This was home.

There had been so many times when he was serving overseas, in the heat and the desert, trying to patch up wounded soldiers who were flown in from the front lines, that all he'd been able to think about was the mountain with the snow cap. The blue, blue water.

And of Christine. Only she'd never seemed to miss him. Maybe that should have been an indicator that rushing into marriage with her hadn't been the best idea. That was her reasoning when he'd come home and found out that she wanted a divorce.

We were too young, Luke. You were going to medical school and you were my first. You were safe. Anthony understands me. We don't have anything in common, Luke. When you were gone he was here. He was always here. I can rely on him...

His smile instantly vanished. Just thinking about

Christine and the heartache that she and Anthony caused him ruined the moment.

This was why he couldn't get involved with someone. This was why he was single and kept people at a distance. You couldn't trust people. It was too painful.

"You know, there's a bear on the loose still and you're on a trail that is an avalanche risk."

Sarah lowered her camera and stared at him in shock and there was a touch of annoyance there, as well.

"What're you doing here?" she asked.

"Didn't you hear me? There's a bear out there on the loose."

She paled. "Wait, I thought you caught it."

"Who told you that?"

"The woman at the rental chalet. She said, and I quote, 'I think he caught him or something. Yeah, yeah, he caught it.'"

Luke rolled his eyes. "Well, that explains it. I spoke to a clueless guy. He really doesn't know much."

"Apparently so. I would've never come out here had I known. I really thought the bear issue was a moot point. I figured since I hadn't seen you for a couple days that you'd dealt with it. I thought you'd gone back up into the woods like you do all the time."

"I understand the woods. I'm used to them. I live in the woods."

She cocked an eyebrow. "Really?"

He nodded. "I have a cabin in the woods. It's on the edge of my parents' property. I built it myself."

"Wow, I'm impressed. I mean, I figured you were a bit of a hands-on guy, but I had no idea that you could build a home with your own hands. That's amazing."

"Thanks. Well, when I got back from my tour of duty

I had a bit of free time." Then he cursed inwardly, because again just a simple twist in the conversation and he was opening up to her again. How did she manage to do that? He was worried that she would try to turn the conversation back to his time overseas. Something that was off-limits.

"Well, it's quite impressive. Most surgeons I know wouldn't risk damaging their hands by doing something like that."

"I'm not like most surgeons. I'm not traditional in any sense of the word." Besides, he didn't practice much surgery anymore. He missed it, but he loved this more. He loved what he did in Crater Lake.

"That's for sure." She smiled and then looked away, aiming her camera at the mountains.

"Didn't you hear me say there's a bear on the loose?"

"I did, but I just want a couple more shots."

A couple more shots? The woman was infuriating.

"So why are you up here?"

"Taking pictures."

"I thought you didn't like the cold?" Luke asked.

"I don't, but it was a beautiful day."

"So what do you do with the pictures?"

She grinned. "I paint a bit."

She paints?

Now it was his turn to be impressed. He hadn't thought she had any hobbies beyond what he'd seen, and that hadn't been much. He'd thought she was a career-focused surgeon. Usually young surgeons didn't have the time for much else—they were too focused on honing their craft.

It pleasantly surprised him.

"Paint?"

Sarah nodded. "I have hidden depths, too."

Luke laughed. "I guess you do. I build homes and you paint."

"I wouldn't mind seeing it sometime."

His blood heated at her suggestion. The thought of her in his home was definitely a dangerous idea, but not all that unpleasant. Luke cleared his throat. "Maybe sometime, but really we have to get down off the trail. Until I find that bear, I really can't authorize people being out here alone and unarmed."

"I brought that can of deterrent."

He smiled at her briefly. "That won't be enough to dissuade a hungry bear just fresh out of torpor."

Sarah sighed. "You're right."

"Come on, I brought my snowmobile, so at least you don't have to hike the entire way back. Even if it would be good practice for you."

She glared at him as she packed her camera carefully back in its case and into her knapsack. "Ha-ha."

"Glad to see you were taking my advice about the backpack."

"Good advice is good advice. Though I'm a bit worried about avalanches. Do those happen a lot up here?"

Luke nodded. "They do. We can do a little simulation if you'd like?"

Sarah groaned. "Fine, but as long as it's inside."

"I promise. I wouldn't want to risk causing an avalanche out here."

Sarah had been surprised to hear Luke's voice from behind her. She hadn't seen him in a couple of days since the mauling. Every time she seemed to get a little bit closer to him, he turned tail and ran into the woods.

Of course, she didn't mind. It was better they had that separation.

She barely knew anything about him and really she shouldn't care all that much, but she wanted to get to know him. Maybe because she was alone here in Crater Lake. She didn't know anyone apart from Luke and a few employees that she greeted in passing at the resort. Then again, when had she really had any friends?

Her whole medical career, heck, her whole life, she hadn't had much time to form any interactions or friendships. And that was the way she wanted it. Her parents had tried to put Sarah into the same activities as her sister. It was just Sarah never really was social. She'd preferred science camp or painting class over tennis camp. She'd been so focused trying to prove to her parents she could do the things she wanted to do, she hadn't made many friends.

Or at least friends who were interested in the same things as she was.

The last date she'd been on the previous year had been so unremarkable. The guy had been handsome, well-to-do, but boring and very full of himself.

Luke was cocky, confident, but there was a difference. He didn't think he was a god. He didn't think he was better than anyone else. He actually tried to help people around him, even if he didn't want people to know that he cared, which she didn't get.

And most of all, he didn't date her because of who her father was.

"You ready?" Luke asked as he straddled the snowmobile.

"I don't have a helmet."

He reached into his knapsack and tossed her one. "There you go. Now get on."

"Do you have furniture in there? Is it like a bottomless bag?"

He chuckled. "Perhaps. You know my motto is be ready for anything."

Sarah laughed and put on her helmet, climbing on the snowmobile behind him. Suddenly she was very nervous about being so close to Luke. Which was ridiculous. They were just coworkers. They weren't even friends.

He's the closest thing you have to a friend.

Which was true and that thought scared her.

"You need to hold on," Luke said over his shoulder.

"Right." Her heart was pounding and she was very aware about how close she was to him. Though she couldn't feel his skin, she was pressed against him enough to feel the hard muscles under all the thick layers of his snowsuit.

At least that was something. There was a wall of protection between the two of them, but for one brief moment she wished there weren't and she couldn't help but wonder what it would be like to be wrapped up in his arms.

Where did that come from?

She shook that thought away, because she couldn't think like that.

Luke was off-limits.

She just held on tight and tried not to think about it. She had to shake the idea of Luke out of her mind. This was her chance to prove to her parents that she didn't need their help to survive. She didn't need anyone's help. She was here because of her own merit. She'd earned the right to be here and she was going to prove to everyone she had the right to be here.

Nothing was going to get in her way.

This was her chance and she had to focus on making this clinic the best. She had to be the best, so there was no time to think about Luke or what might be.

She didn't have time for romance. She couldn't lose her focus and if she got involved with Luke, she probably would. He was so gorgeous, so delicious and so very distracting.

This job was too important to her. Her parents had scoffed when she'd turned down the job her father had got for her and taken this one. They believed she would fail and come back to them with her proverbial tail between her legs.

This job won't wait for you, Sarah. I pulled a lot of strings for you.

She couldn't let them think that way. They might not think she could handle this, but she could.

Luke was not for her, even if she wished she could indulge. She had to be strong around him, keep him at a distance and remember why she was here.

She wasn't here to fall in love. That wasn't in the cards for her.

She was here to be a doctor. She was here to run the most prestigious private clinic in northwest Montana.

This job was her chance, because, even though everything about her medical career had been handed to her, according to her father she was a damn good doctor.

She was a damn good surgeon.

Are you sure about that?

They pulled up to the resort and Luke parked his snowmobile away from the main entrance. When the engine was off, Sarah clambered off the snowmobile, her legs shaking from the ride.

"That was my first and last snowmobile ride, I think," she said, trying to make light of the situation. She handed Luke back the helmet. "Thanks for being prepared."

"No problem. Now, no going back out onto the trails until that bear has been subdued."

"I hope you don't have to kill it."

Luke frowned. "I hope the bear returns to its den, but I doubt it. The game warden is combing the mountains, as well."

"Thanks again for coming to get me. I hope I didn't ruin your day."

"You didn't ruin it, but you put a serious dent in my plans." He winked at her.

"You're an idiot."

Luke was going to say something more, but they were interrupted when a front-desk person came running out of the side door.

"Thank goodness I found you both," she said. "There's an emergency up in Suite 501."

"What's wrong?" Sarah asked.

"A guest has gone into labor."

Luke's eyes widened. "Well, that's something I've never dealt with."

"Really?"

"Not many pregnant soldiers on the front line."

"Well, perhaps I can teach you something." Sarah turned to the front-desk woman. "Get her comfortable, call the air ambulance and tell them we'll be there in ten minutes."

The woman nodded and disappeared back inside.

"You've seriously delivered a baby before?" Luke asked with a hint of admiration in his voice.

"I'm a surgeon and part of the training was a rotation on the obstetrical rounds. I can do this."

"I'm sure you can. Not sure I can."

She grinned. "After today you will. Come on."

Luke nodded and they headed inside.

Sarah didn't want to tell him that she was nervous, too. She hadn't delivered that many babies, but right now she didn't have a choice. She couldn't be nervous. There was a job to do.

There were two lives to save.

CHAPTER FIVE

"COME ON, ONE more push," Sarah urged. "You can do it."

It had been a long time since she'd delivered a baby. She had been nervous for a moment, hoping she'd remember how.

As a trauma surgeon she didn't see many births. When a pregnant woman came into the ER Sarah would look at them briefly before an OB/GYN was called, but the moment she'd checked on the mother at the hotel everything she'd learned had come back to her.

Which was a good thing. This patient needed her.

Luke was behind the mother, holding her up, helping her. The air ambulance had arrived, but by the time they arrived there was no way they could move the mother. The baby was on the way out and moving the mother would put the baby at risk.

"You're doing great," Luke reassured the woman.

Sarah smiled up at him, but he wasn't looking at her. Instead he was focused on helping their patient and it warmed her heart. He could've stood back because he admitted that he didn't know anything about childbirth, but instead he threw himself into the work.

He was gentle. Kind.

For a man that was referred to around the hotel as a

lone wolf, keeping people at bay, disappearing into his cabin up in the woods, Luke had a large amount of tenderness to him. It made her chest tighten just a little bit.

There was something about a rough, tough exterior and a gentle hand. It made him endearing.

The mother let out a loud yell and Sarah gently helped the baby girl into the world. Sarah rubbed the baby's back and soon the newborn was crying lustily.

"Good job," Sarah encouraged.

The mom laid back and Luke came over to help her. He was grinning ear to ear as he handed her sterile scissors.

"Good job, Doctor," he whispered in her ear. It sent a tingle down her spine.

She didn't say anything as she cut the umbilical cord and then wrapped the baby up in a blanket and handed her to Luke so he could give her to the mother.

"Congratulations, Mom," Luke said as he carefully transferred the baby to her mother's arms. He glanced down at the tiny girl as he did so, those blue eyes twinkling as he gently cradled her. So little in his big hands. It made Sarah's heart skip a beat.

Having a family had never been on her radar. Maybe because she'd had such a lonely childhood, even with a sister. They were raised by nannies in the old archaic "children should be seen and not heard" style.

How could she even contemplate raising a family when she didn't even know how one was supposed to function?

So she'd never entertained the idea, but in this moment, watching the joy on the mother's face, she yearned for something more.

"She's beautiful," Luke said.

The mother cried tears of joy and exhaustion as she took the small bundle from Luke. It was this moment that Sarah had always enjoyed when she'd been a resident and worked the obstetrical round. The moment of pure joy and elation. The moment when mother and child met. It could warm even the coldest hearts.

And watching Luke hold that small child melted hers completely.

What was it about him?

Most of the time he drove her completely around the bend, but there were times like this, when he was dealing with patients, that made her soften toward him. She wanted to get to know him and she never wanted to get to know anyone. What was it about him?

He's a mystery.

And maybe that was why she was so drawn to him. He was a challenge and she'd never backed down from a challenge before.

You need to back down from this one.

Sarah tore her gaze away from Luke and turned back to the patient. The paramedics stood at the ready. Even though the birth had been simple, mother and baby still had to be taken to the nearest hospital to be checked out.

Once she was finished the paramedics stepped in and started to get ready to transfer the patients. Her job was done. She cleaned up the mess and put it in a trash bag that she would take down to her medical-waste receptacle in her clinic.

Now you're picking up trash? Sarah, you weren't raised to do that.

You can't be an obstetrician. I didn't pay for your medical schooling so you can do obstetrics.

She hated the way her parents' voices were always

in her head, trying to control her. For a long time she'd managed to tune them out, right up until she'd discovered what her father had done.

Now they were constantly there, questioning her every move.

Sarah would've liked to have been an OB/GYN surgeon, but her father didn't think it was dignified enough. Of course, he hadn't been too pleased when she gave up training to be a cardio-thoracic surgeon under Dr. Eli Draven, but Sarah preferred general surgery. She preferred trauma surgery.

Most people thought that general and trauma surgery was boring, but it wasn't. It was exciting. She got to work on so much with general surgery, and as a trauma surgeon she saw everything, but still she'd kind of missed her chance on working with mothers and babies.

Even though she'd always stressed that she didn't want to get married, that she wanted to focus on her career, there had always been a part of her that wanted the family she hadn't had as a child.

Sarah had grown up in wealth and privilege. She'd wanted for nothing except love and admiration from her parents. Maybe even to spend some time with them.

Watching this mother dote on her new baby made her wonder if her own mother had ever looked at her that way before, and seeing Luke smile so tenderly at them made her yearn.

In this moment she longed for something more.

She just didn't think that was possible.

Not in the near future anyway. Probably never.

Luke came over and peeled off his gloves and threw them in the bag, interrupting her train of thought.

"Good job, Dr. Ledet."

She chuckled. “I really didn’t do much. The mother did all the work.”

He smiled at her. “Still, you did a good job nonetheless. I would’ve been totally lost.”

“What about your brother? He’s the town doctor, doesn’t he deliver babies?”

“He does, but he lives in town. That’s at least a twenty-minute drive in this weather. He wouldn’t have made it in time.”

“No,” she agreed. “That baby was coming quickly.”

They moved out of the way as the paramedics passed them.

“Thank you, Doctors,” the mother said, grinning ear to ear.

“Congratulations,” Sarah said. “Everything will be okay.”

Sarah watched as they wheeled her patient and the baby out of the suite. It had been so wonderful being a part of that moment, watching a family being formed. Being part of their love. She was sad to watch them go.

She sighed. “Well, that was certainly exciting.”

“It was, but I don’t understand it.”

“What don’t you understand?”

“I don’t understand why a woman so close to delivering decided to come up here on a ski trip,” Luke said as he moved away from her.

“I think it was a family trip. Perhaps she would’ve been left home alone. I think it was a good thing she was here.”

He nodded. “Yeah. You’re probably right.”

Sarah knotted the trash bag and glanced around the suite. “I feel bad for Housekeeping, but honestly I think that mattress is no good anymore.”

"That's the first birth I've attended. I mean, besides my own."

"You've never attended one in medical school?"

He shook his head. "I did most of my training in the army. My residency was in Germany at a hospital there. So not only do I speak fluent French, I speak fluent German, too."

"You're a man of many trades, Dr. Ralston."

"I have a lot of secrets." Then he grinned and winked at her in a way that made her heart skip a beat. She had to get out of the room. She had to put some distance between them.

"I'm sure you do, but I have to take this to the clinic." She held up the garbage bag.

"When are you going to show me your paintings?"

The question caught her off guard. Any time anything had ever gotten too personal between them, he'd disappeared into the woods. So when he asked about her paintings, it shocked her.

No one had ever asked to see her paintings before. And she never told anyone about them. If he hadn't caught her taking photographs, she wouldn't have told him. Most people thought her art and pursuing it was silly.

Again, another dream her parents quashed really fast.

They're called starving artists for a reason, Sarah.

Her mother hadn't wanted her to be an artist, and yet her mother had supported the local arts scene in New York City. Bought paintings, attended galas and gallery openings. Then again, that was what women like her mother did. It was *the* thing to do in her parents' circles.

"You want to see my paintings?"

"Sure. You said you take pictures and then do paintings. I'm interested. I've never met a doctor who painted landscapes or drew or anything for that matter."

Sarah chuckled. "It's good for the hands. Especially surgeon hands. Keeps them strong."

"So, when do I get to see them?"

"I don't know. When do I get to see the house you built?" Then the blood drained away from her face when she realized what she'd just done. This was not keeping him at a distance. This was inviting him in.

"How about tonight?" he asked, surprising her.

"Tonight?"

"You have plans tonight?"

"No."

He nodded then, those blue eyes twinkling with something she wasn't sure of, but it made her heart beat a bit faster.

"Okay, then, so you'll come to my place tonight. I'll see some of your paintings and you can see my handiwork."

"Okay." Sarah looked away and hoped that she wasn't blushing. "I better get this to medical waste."

"I'll pick you up at seven."

She nodded and didn't look back at him. She couldn't, because if she did then he would see how he was affecting her.

Damn him.

And then she cursed herself a bit, wondering what the heck she'd just gotten herself into.

What have I done?

Luke had repeatedly asked himself that since he'd invited Sarah over to his house. He didn't have anyone at his house. Ever.

Only Carson and that was rare. Usually when Luke got together with Carson he went to Carson's place.

It was larger.

Luke went for the understated. An open-concept cabin. Carson referred to it as a shack, as if Luke were some kind of prospector up in Alaska on a gold claim.

Everything in the cabin he'd made. Well, the furniture anyway. So what if he preferred to live off the grid a bit? He wasn't totally off the grid. He had electricity and running water. No, he didn't have a phone or cable, but he had a radio if he ever got into trouble or if someone wanted to reach him.

There wasn't any cell phone reception where his cabin was and he still hadn't quite figured out why. Probably all the pine trees around it.

Christine had hated this cabin when he'd planned it. Even though it did have creature comforts like a sauna out back and a nice bathroom. Everything was too "rough" for her.

When he picked Sarah up at the hotel, he was actually hoping that she would make up an excuse and cop out, but she didn't. She was waiting for him at the front in her coat with a black portfolio slung over her shoulder.

He had no choice but to live up to his end of the bargain and take her to his home. The truck ride over was tense, because he didn't know what to say to her. All he could think about on the journey was how he was going to get out of this situation. A situation that was his fault. He only had himself to blame.

When he'd told Carson what he'd done, he'd thought his brother had witnessed a miracle healing the way his mouth had dropped open.

"You don't date. You said so yourself and you repeatedly made fun of me when I got together with Esme."

"It's not a date. She's a coworker."

Carson had grinned, smugly. "You keep telling yourself that, my friend. You're not fooling me."

Luke had decided he didn't need Carson's advice, called his brother a few choice names and left. Carson was certainly making him eat crow and maybe he deserved it just a bit, because he'd certainly given Carson a run for his money when Esme had started coming around more often.

Still, that was a completely different situation.

Carson was in love with Esme.

Luke wasn't interested in Sarah. Not in that way.

Liar.

This was a dangerous situation. They were in his cabin, in the woods and they were alone. That wasn't a good combo. His self-control was going to be tested tonight, because any time he was around her it was tested.

All he wanted to do was kiss those pink lips, to run his hands through her blond hair and hold her in his arms, to feel her body pressed against his.

Don't think about her like that. She's not yours. She can't be yours. That's not what you want.

Only the more he tried to convince himself of that the harder it was for him to believe it.

"Wow, so this is it?" Sarah asked as he parked his truck in front of his cabin.

"Yes, this is my shack, as my brother calls it."

"Well, at least it'll be warm. I can see you left the home fires burning."

"Yes, I have electricity, but my house is heated by my

wood stove. I live a bit off the grid, as much as I can. I like to rough it."

"Do you grow your own food, too?" She was teasing him.

"No, I don't really have a green thumb. I forage mostly. Our dinner tonight will be moss and various pine needles."

She laughed. "Well, can we go inside? I'd like to see this old shack you built."

"Ha-ha." They climbed out of the truck and he opened the door for her. She stepped in first and stood in the small mudroom of his cabin. She was silent and he found himself starting to sweat, waiting for her approval.

Probably because the last time he'd shown a woman his place it had been Christine and she'd hated it and then it had been only the schematics and blueprints.

You expect me to live here?

You wanted a house when I was done with my tours. I'm building this for us.

Don't think about her.

She wasn't going to intrude into his thoughts. Not tonight.

"Well?" he asked, trying not to seem too anxious. "What do you think?"

"It's beautiful. I'm pretty impressed that you built this place." She took off her coat and hung it on the hooks that he had in the entranceway and then kicked off her boots and stepped on the thick Berber area rug that he had in the living-cum-bedroom area of his home. "The furniture seems to match the house perfectly."

"It should, I made it."

She cocked her eyebrows. "You made the furniture, too?"

He nodded. "Everything. Even the mattress."

Why did I say that?

Pink stained her cheeks when he said mattress, but she wouldn't look in the direction of the king-size bed that he'd built in the far corner. Seeing how he affected her made his own blood heat. Since she'd dropped into his arms in her office a couple weeks back, there had been countless times that he'd pictured her naked in his bed, her legs wrapped around his waist.

What he wouldn't give to peel that pale pink boatneck sweater and those tight blue jeans from her body, to run his hands over her soft skin.

Get a grip on yourself.

He cleared his throat and ran his hand through his hair nervously.

"Yeah, I made the mattress out of feathers I'd collected over time. It used to be a straw tick, but that was quite uncomfortable."

"This isn't *Little House on the Prairie*, Pa."

He laughed with her and it defused the tension. He headed into the kitchen. "Would you like a glass of wine?"

"Did you press the grapes yourself?" she teased, setting her portfolio down on his coffee table.

"No. I do go to the grocery store from time to time. I'm not Davy Crockett."

"Could've fooled me." There was a twinkle in her eyes and she leaned over his counter. "I didn't expect dinner or drinks. I thought you were showing me your handiwork and I was going to show you some of mine."

He shrugged. "I rarely have dinner guests. I'm a bit of a Grinch around these parts."

"So I've heard."

"Who did you hear that from?" he asked.

"I went into town on my first week. Met a woman with these two twins and they mentioned how cantankerous you were. I had to agree with them at the time."

Luke groaned. "The Johnstone twins. Yes, they're not fond of me and I'm not too fond of them."

"Why? They looked like innocent enough children."

Luke snorted. "They delight in spooking my horse."

"You have a horse?"

He nodded. "I board her in a stable close to town in the winter. In the summer I have a pad out back that I keep her in. She can't handle the deep snow up here in the winter. She is getting on in years, sadly."

"You have hidden depths, Dr. Ralston."

You have no idea.

Only he didn't say that out loud. Instead he pulled down two wineglasses from where they were hanging on the wall and set them down before her.

"I'm afraid I only have white, but I think white will do well with the salmon I'm making."

"Salmon?"

"I smoked it myself."

She grinned. "I should've known. White is fine."

He pulled the only bottle he had in his house and uncorked it, pouring it into her glass and then his. He wasn't much of a wine drinker, but Esme really liked wine and so he figured Sarah would, too, but she took a sip and made a face.

"What's wrong?" he asked. "Did it go bad?"

"No, it's fine. It's just…I'm not much of a wine drinker. I like beer instead."

Now it was his turn to be shocked. "Who has hidden depths?"

She laughed. "My mother would be horrified if she

knew that I was telling a man this. I was brought up to be prim and proper. I was not brought up to be a roughneck."

"A what?" he asked.

"My mother is from a very proper British family. A roughneck is someone who works offshore in oil or gas. Tough, rugged, dirty. I was meant to be refined and graceful."

"You're a bit of a klutz. I don't think you're all that graceful. I have seen you face-first in a snowdrift."

She laughed again and it warmed his heart to hear it. She had an infectious laugh and he couldn't remember the last time he'd felt so at ease around a woman before. Usually he was hiding behind his wall, but not at this moment. He was exposed and he didn't like that one bit.

What was she doing to him?

Sarah didn't know what she was expecting when Luke brought her out to his cabin. She must've been thinking more of a barren shack. Even though his home was rustic, it wasn't barren. It was cozy. It was homey.

It was the kind of place people from the city rented when they went on ski trips. The only difference was it would probably be larger. It was a little too small for most people, but she kind of liked it.

She was shocked that he made most of the furniture in the home, though she seriously doubted he made the leather L-shaped couch that was in the living room adorned with pillows and a polar fleece throw.

Then her gaze drifted off to the bed in the far corner of the open-concept cabin. It was a large wooden four-poster bed with a thick, down-and-feather-filled mattress. Well, according to him it was.

He made his own mattress?

She shook her head. Stop thinking about the bed.

He was in the kitchen checking on the salmon, his back to her. He'd handed her a beer a few moments ago and then gone about cooking the rest of dinner, leaving her to her own devices and the naughty thoughts that were running through her mind.

She sat down on the couch and tried to ignore the large bed, which felt like an elephant in the room at the moment.

Don't think about it. This is just dinner as friends.

Luke came out of the kitchen, holding a bottle of beer. "Just a little bit longer. Sorry about that."

She shrugged. "I didn't expect dinner tonight. It's a nice surprise."

"After all your hard work today, it was the least I could do."

"I just did my job."

"Yeah and you did a good job." Luke picked up her portfolio. "Do you mind if I look?"

"Go ahead. I am at your mercy." Blood rushed to her cheeks.

Luke grinned at her, that devious grin that made her insides turn to goo. "Well, let's see your artistic abilities."

Sarah's pulse thundered in her ears as he thumbed through her very small portfolio. It was something she'd never shown anyone before. It was something she'd always felt she couldn't share with someone, but Luke had caught her in the act.

And she couldn't lie to him.

Or she didn't want to lie to him, but now she was regretting it because he wasn't saying much. What if he hated it? What if she sucked at it?

Who cares?

Only she did care. She cared if he hated it. What he thought mattered to her and that scared her.

"These are great. Where was this one done?" He held up a picture of the Black Hills. She'd spent some time around Mount Rushmore when she was a kid. That picture was something that she'd painted from memory, because that trip to Mount Rushmore with her parents was one of her last happy memories. They weren't this socialite family, they were just like everyone else. Except her father had rented a massive cabin on the outskirts of Keystone on this huge ranch that had horses and tennis courts, but still it was a happy time in her life.

"The Black Hills."

Luke glanced at it again. "South Dakota?"

She nodded. "Yes. Keystone, South Dakota."

"Yes, now I see it. I like South Dakota."

"You've been there?"

"Who hasn't? It's like Mecca for American families of our generation. Plus, it's not too far away for a family doctor to take his family for a summer vacation. My father was the only town physician in Crater Lake for a long time, so any vacation had to be taken in a drivable radius to home. Where did your family vacation, other than Mount Rushmore?"

"Jamaica, Brazil… India."

He raised an eyebrow. "Have you been around the world?"

"Pretty much." She took a swig of her beer. "My last job, teaching at different hospitals, took me to a lot of places, too. That's why I was in Missoula that day."

"Teaching?"

She nodded. "I worked with a surgeon who was developing a new technique in robotic trauma surgery. It was a good job."

"Why did you give it up?"

Her stomach twisted as she thought about those last moments. About when she'd found out that the job she'd been working on so hard hadn't really been something she'd earned.

It still made her angry.

"You look tense."

"I don't like to talk about the past too much." She set her beer down on the table. "Maybe I should head back to the hotel. I'm not that hungry."

"You're staying. I'm sorry, I won't pry." He set the portfolio down on the table. "Besides, I think it's done."

She watched as he walked into the kitchen. Why did he have to pry into her history? He didn't share his.

What was she doing here?

You're lonely.

She should just leave. It would be better if she left, only she couldn't.

She was a bit of a masochist.

"Have a seat at the table and I'll bring you dinner."

Sarah picked up her beer and headed over to the dining-room table, sitting down at the end. "Don't tell me you made this too?"

"Yep. I told you. I made most of the furniture here." He came out of the kitchen with two plates and set down in front of her a perfectly cooked filet of salmon, asparagus and new potatoes. It smelled delicious. "For a long time since I returned from the army, I didn't practice medicine and all I wanted to do was build stuff for my home."

"Why?" she asked.

He frowned and she knew she was treading on that dangerous ground. That moment when he would clam up. "I needed time."

"I get that."

He shrugged, but he didn't say anything else and an awkward silence fell between them. She wished that he would open up and share with her, but then again she wasn't exactly sharing much with him either.

So they were at a standstill.

And maybe that was for the best.

After dinner, she helped him clean up, though he insisted that wasn't necessary. Then they returned to the couch in his living room, where he continued to look at her paintings and drawings. As he was skimming through he found one that absolutely captivated him. It was a self-portrait she'd done and by the date on the bottom it was a few years ago. It took his breath away. The details in the drawing. It was just a pencil sketch, but there was so much life to it.

The kissable lips, heart-shaped face, nose that turned up again, thinly arched brows and beautiful eyes that captured him. In the portrait her hair hung loose over bare shoulders, like wisps. Usually she wore it back in a braid and tonight it was done up in a bun. He resisted the urge to undo that bun and let her hair cascade down all over her shoulders. So he could kiss and hold that woman in the picture. It was as if the drawing showed a hidden part of her.

The true Sarah.

And he longed to know the true Sarah, which scared him.

"Which one are you looking at so intently?"

Luke quickly flicked the page. "Uh, this one. The horse on the plains. It's beautiful."

She smiled. "You can have it if you want."

"Thanks."

The horse one was good. It actually reminded him of his own horse, who he hadn't seen in a couple of days, but he'd rather keep the pencil-drawn self-portrait she'd done.

Why torture yourself?

"You said you have a horse?"

"Yeah. I do."

"What's its name?"

"Her name is Adele."

"That's an interesting choice."

"Well, I didn't really choose it. When I bought her that was her name. I didn't see a point in changing it."

"I love horseback riding." Sarah sighed. "I miss it."

"You know how to horseback ride?"

She nodded. "Regular lessons. One thing I didn't mind my parents pressuring me into."

"Your parents have a large impact on your life?" he asked.

She frowned and then shrugged. "What parents don't?"

"True," Luke agreed, but there was something more to what she'd said about her parents. He wanted to press her further, but decided against it.

He didn't mind this friendly chatter or when they worked so well together when faced with a medical emergency. Anything else was risky and he didn't want her to find a way in. He set down his glass.

"You know, I haven't seen her in a long time. I've been so busy. I should go check on her. Would you like to come?"

Her eyes lit up, as if he were offering her a thousand dollars.

"Really?"

He nodded. "Really."

"I would love that."

"Grab your coat." He handed her back the portfolio. "After I check on her I'll take you back to the hotel."

It was a short drive to the stable where he kept Adele. The owner of the stable was used to Luke keeping odd hours and didn't mind that Luke was here to visit his horse at eleven in the evening.

As they got out of the car a brilliant set of northern lights erupted across the sky, because the cloud cover that had been hovering over Crater Lake the past few days had dissipated.

"Oh, my God!" Sarah said, a cloud of breath escaping past her lips. "Look at that."

"Pretty spectacular, isn't it?"

"I've never seen one. Too much light pollution."

"I can imagine that. Cities are so ugly."

She shook her head. "New York isn't ugly. The lights are beautiful. Especially around the holidays like Christmas and Valentine's Day. They light up the Empire State Building and then at Christmas there's this large tree at Rockefeller Square."

Luke wrinkled his nose. "Christmas sounds fine. Valentine's, why even bother? Besides, light pollution has nothing on this. Look straight up."

Sarah leaned back and he watched as her expression turned from amusement to awe. Now that the cloud cover was gone there were millions of stars splattered across the sky. As if Van Gogh's *Starry Night* were painted across the inky black sky.

"Amazing."

He smiled at her as he watched her stare up in amazement at the star-filled sky. He remembered so many times, after working on soldiers for countless hours, walking out of the OR and standing in the dark, staring up at the sky in Afghanistan and wishing for this.

The night sky was different.

And there was no aurora borealis.

Afghanistan's sky was beautiful, silent and cold at night, but nothing beat Montana, the mountains. Nothing beat home.

And in this moment, he wanted to take Sarah in his arms and kiss her. The urge was undeniable and he had to regain control before he did something he would regret.

Who said you'd regret it?

"Come on, I don't want you to catch your death out here. Adele won't like it too much if your teeth are chattering the whole time."

They walked into the stable and as soon as he did Adele stuck her head out of the stall, watching him.

"She knows you're here."

Luke grinned. "I know, but really she's just looking for treats."

"I don't know about that."

Luke's blood heated at her teasing tone, but he didn't acknowledge it; instead he cleared his throat and pulled out Adele's carrot treat.

"Hey, girl," he whispered against her muzzle. "How have they been treating you?"

"I'd love to paint her. She's beautiful."

"Come pet her. She doesn't mind. What she minds is people spooking her."

"Can you blame her?" Sarah asked and then she approached Adele slowly. Adele moved her head slightly, not used to the stranger who was about to touch her.

"It's okay, Adele. This is a friend. Another doctor."

Adele nickered and Sarah was able to stroke her muzzle.

"You're so beautiful, Adele," Sarah whispered.

Luke watched Sarah stroke and touch his horse, and his heart, which he'd thought was safely encased in ice, began to melt for her. She was like no other woman he'd ever met and his blood burned with the need to possess her. To have her for his own.

You can't have her.

"She's beautiful, Luke. So beautiful. I would love to ride her one day, if you'd let me."

Luke cleared his throat. "We'll see. I better get you back to your hotel. It's getting late."

"Sure." Sarah leaned forward and kissed Adele. "Good night, beauty."

And at that moment Luke knew he'd have to put some serious distance between the two of them, or he was liable to carry her off and make love to her.

Right now.

CHAPTER SIX

"YOU'RE A SADIST—you know that, right?"

Luke just grinned at her, as he stood over her in the snow. Gone was the gentle soul of a man she'd seen last night in that horse stable, the gentle giant cradling that fragile infant. That man made her ache with need. She craved him like air, but this guy, torturing her with endless simulations, this guy she wanted to club upside the head.

He'd taken her outside to where the snow plows had been piling the snow from the parking lot. The large snowbank was littered with CPR dummies, half-buried. It was a simulation massacre.

Only he'd dubbed this as avalanche training.

"I thought we were going to do avalanche training inside?"

"How would that work?" he asked.

"We could pretend. Use our imagination."

"We were, until I found this snow pile. It's perfect."

"Great," she mumbled.

"You need to work harder to dig this man out."

Sarah rolled her eyes. "I'm just a hotel doctor. I'm not going to be the first line of defense called for this. You are, your brother probably and every other first responder up here on this mountain."

"You'll be called, too. In situations like this, everyone with medical training will be called into action. That's how it works up in these remote communities. Are you saying that you're not going to come to an avalanche site because you're just a hotel doctor?"

Damn.

He was right. She wouldn't walk away from an emergency situation. She was a doctor and she was trained in trauma, just as he was.

"Fine." She kept digging away at the snow.

"Use your ice axe, too. Chip away at the hard stuff. Just don't hit the patient."

Sarah made a face at him and he just laughed.

"Do you think you can insert a chest tube in below-zero temps?"

"You're not serious, are you?"

"You said you worked in an ER. Haven't you inserted chest tubes before?"

"Of course," Sarah said. "But not in the bitter cold. Usually when I insert a chest tube it's in a trauma pod, sheltered and indoors."

Not negative eighty with a windchill.

"Ah, but sometimes there's no time to get the man down off the mountain and you have to do it in the field." Luke reached into his knapsack and pulled out a chest-tube kit. "Insert a chest tube. The patient's lungs are filling with blood—he needs a chest tube."

Sarah pulled off her mitts and fumbled with the chest-tube tray. She hadn't realized how cold her fingers actually were, but then she remembered that they'd been out here for an hour already while he went through avalanche drills with her.

The mitts were warm, but, after a while digging in the snow, their protective lining couldn't keep out the bitter cold forever. She cursed under her breath, as she prepared the chest tube and inserted it perfectly the first time.

She had always been pretty good at it.

"Good job," Luke remarked. "Now put on your gloves and keep digging."

"I need a break."

"You don't get a break on the mountain."

"This isn't a mountain. It's the snow from the main parking lot and as you can see we're the current entertainment." She pointed to the window where staff and a few guests were watching them cavorting on top of the dirty snowbank, with mannequins strewn everywhere.

"It's mandatory training, but I suppose you can have a break. You were up late last night."

Sarah smiled and tried not to blush as she thought about it. She actually hadn't wanted the night to end, though it had been for the best. If it hadn't ended she might have done something foolish, like kiss him, and maybe that one foolish kiss would have led to something more.

So it was good that the night had ended when it had.

Still, she couldn't remember when she'd had such a good time. "Yes, thanks for the fantastic dinner and the conversation. I enjoyed it."

"Me, too," he said, but then the small smile that he had for her quickly disappeared and he got up, to walk slowly down the side of the snowbank.

For a while after their awkward conversation it was pretty quiet, but then he started asking about her art and her photographs, then the tension melted away. Still, at the mention of last night the atmosphere changed and put distance between them. Maybe he was regretting last night. She certainly hoped not.

He was the closest thing she had to a friend in Crater Lake. Loneliness had never bothered her before, but that was probably because she'd been busier as a surgeon. There were guests at the hotel, but not many as the grand opening was only a couple of weeks away on Valentine's Day and, even then, guests weren't always getting sick.

So far, since her arrival in Crater Lake, she'd treated about eight sunburns, three cases of some gastroenteritis, a bear mauling and a birth of a baby. And because she wasn't as busy as she was in her previous job, she had a lot more free time. A lot more time to remind her that she was alone.

Of course, she didn't really think that if she followed her mother and sister in their footsteps that she would feel any different. Her society friends weren't really friends at all.

None of them had called her since she'd decided to cut ties with New York and move to Montana. Actually, they'd been quite horrified when she'd told them she'd given up the prestigious job and was moving to Crater Lake.

Who cares if your father pulled strings? My father did, too. It doesn't matter.

It matters to me, Nikki. My father doesn't think I can do anything. He's thinks I'm this baby. He thinks I'm helpless. I need to do this on my own.

Thinking about that last conversation with her so-called best friend made her blood pressure rise. It made her angry. It made her remember that she wasn't sure if anything in her life was her own. She wasn't sure if she'd earned anything.

It was humiliating.

Don't think about it. Don't give them the time of day.

"Do you have avalanches here every year?" she asked, hoping that the conversation could turn in another direction and distract her. It would keep her mind off her parents, her so-called friends and Luke.

"Pretty much."

"To this extent?"

Luke shook his head. "No, thankfully we haven't had a major disaster like this in a long, long time, but being in a mountainous region there are always avalanches. Always. That's why we have avalanche zones."

"How do you determine what an avalanche zone is?"

Luke clambered back up the snowbank to stand beside her. He pointed toward the mountain. "You see that part of the mountain? You see how it's on a forty-five-degree angle? It's considered an avalanche zone. In fact we had a landslide on that slope last year."

"The landslide that almost killed Shane Draven?"

He nodded. "Yes, Dr. Petersen, my brother and I extracted him and got him down."

"All-hands-on-deck type of situation, then?"

He nodded. "You got it."

"So only steep slopes are considered dangerous."

"No, gradual slopes are at risk, too. And shady slopes can pose a threat."

"Why?" she asked. "Wouldn't the snow harden there as opposed to being in the sun?"

"No, the sun actually hardens the snow better. It melts it and then at night ice forms and seals the snowcap better. Shady slopes don't have that chance—it's just powder."

Sarah shuddered. "I hope we never have a bad avalanche, then. I wouldn't know what to do."

"As long as you're aware of the avalanche zones, you'll be fine, but that's why I'm training you. So you know what to do in an emergency. You can get seriously hurt. I broke my leg during an avalanche last winter. Avalanches are a mighty force. You need to learn how to survive." Luke moved behind her and she was very aware that he was close to her. He touched her arms and, even through all those thick layers, it was electric the way he affected her.

"What're you doing?" she asked, her voice hitching because he was touching her.

He leaned over her shoulder, his hot breath fanning the exposed skin of her neck. "I'm teaching you how to survive if you're ever caught in one. This is Special Forces training now."

"Oh," she said. "How can you fight fast-moving snow?"

"Swim." Then he took her arms and moved them gently in a breaststroke. "If you're ever caught in fast-moving snow, drop your gear because it will weigh you down, open your arms wide and swim to the side of the snow pack. Even if you can't make it across, the movement will help keep your head above the snow so you can breathe."

"Swim through snow?" Sarah smiled. "I've never heard of that before. And what happens if I'm covered with snow?"

"Bring your arms and hands to the front of your face and wiggle back and forth. It will create an air pocket and you'll be able to breathe until help arrives."

"Have you ever been trapped in an avalanche?"

"No, never trapped and never been standing at the edge of an active one. The avalanche I was injured in was because I was rescuing someone. I jumped from a helicopter and landed the wrong way, losing my footing. I've never been trapped, thank God, and I hope I never am."

"I hope so, too." Sarah looked up at him, but his face was unreadable because his sunglasses were covering his eyes, protecting them from snow blindness.

"Thanks." He cleared his throat and moved away from her. "We should get back to freeing these victims."

"Good, 'cause I have big plans this afternoon." She was teasing, but his brow furrowed.

"What kind of plans?"

"I'm going to Crater Lake. I haven't been in town since I first arrived. I have the rest of the day off and I thought I would explore."

"I don't go to town this time of year," Luke remarked.

"Why not?"

"Valentine's Day is coming." He shuddered. "The town is going a little bit crazy about it because of the hotel's grand opening that day. There's going to be a big gala or ball or something."

"I know. Silas Draven is insisting all his employees go, but it sounds kind of fun."

Luke grunted.

"You're not a fan of Valentine's Day?"

"Nope. It's pointless."

"Love is pointless?" she asked.

"No, not pointless just…there's no need to celebrate Valentine's Day with such vigor."

"Why do you hate it so much?" she asked.

He just grunted again, but avoided her question and she wondered why Luke thought love was pointless. She didn't know many guys who actually liked Valentine's Day, but Luke was acting a bit like a Grinch about it.

Why should you care?

And really she shouldn't. When did she ever give two hoots about Valentine's Day before? Usually she was in the hospital, doing surgery and stealing candy from the nurses' station as she went from OR to OR.

She'd never had a Valentine before. Still, the idea of a town getting all decked out and celebrating it sounded as if it could be fun.

"I think it will be fun to see what the town is doing," she said, trying to change the subject before Luke shut down on her again and didn't say anything else.

"Well, have fun. I have to take a group of surveyors out on a trail for some training."

"More surveyors?"

Luke nodded as he headed down the snowbank to their next patient. "I guess some more people are trying to cash in on Silas Draven's bright idea to turn Crater Lake into the next Whitefish."

"I thought you worked exclusively for Silas Draven?" she asked.

He grinned. "No, I'm a free agent. Now come on, get down here so we can save this patient and then we can call it quits for the day."

Sarah groaned but climbed down the snow pile toward him, because she was tired of being in the snow. She was cold and, really, what was the point?

Luke was a closed book.

And that was all there was to it.

Luke had lost his mind. Well, he had for a brief moment there when he'd stepped behind Sarah and touched her.

He didn't know what he'd been thinking about at that moment. Clearly, he was suffering from the cold.

He'd shown other people how to swim out of fast-moving snow and he did that without touching them. He just told them to open their arms wide and mimic swimming, but with Sarah he'd reached out and guided her arms.

And he had no idea why he'd felt the need to do that.

Probably because he liked to torture himself?

Or maybe it was because he couldn't resist her. When he was around her, he wasn't himself. He didn't guard his walls as carefully as he used to. She made him weak. As if she was his Achilles' heel or something.

Yet, like a masochist he kept going back to her. Kept reaching out to her.

She'll hurt you just like Christine did.

He'd done so much for Christine when they were newly married. She'd known he was going to serve in the army, but she hadn't cared. She hadn't wanted to accompany him to Germany, but their marriage had survived. And it had survived his first tour of duty, too.

It was only when she'd demanded he end his career, that he return home to start a family with his wife, that he'd learned she didn't want him.

She didn't want to be his wife.

She'd rather be Anthony's wife, because he'd always been there for her. Unlike him.

I gave up my commission in the army for you.

It was too late for me then, Luke. It was just too late.

You could've come to Germany with me.

You never asked if I wanted to go to Germany. You just said we were moving there and, no, I didn't want to go live in Germany. I didn't want to stay here in Crater Lake either, but it was better than Germany. Of course, my dreams don't matter to you at all. Why couldn't you just open a practice with your father? What was wrong with that? Why couldn't you bend your plans for me or at least ask me if I shared them?

You want me to practice with my father and Carson. Fine. I will.

It's too late, Luke. You were selfish. My desires and wishes never mattered. I'm sorry, but I can't be with you anymore.

This was why he couldn't be near anyone. Why he thought love was pointless. For him anyway. What was the point of falling in love when it could be taken away in an instant?

Carson found love again.

He shook that thought away. That was a different situation. Carson never married Danielle. Carson was never betrayed as Luke was.

There was no room in his heart anymore. He couldn't let there be.

"So what's wrong with this patient?" Sarah used air quotes.

Luke groaned. "Why are you using air quotes? This is a serious situation."

Sarah laughed behind her hand and he couldn't help but smile.

Darn her.

Why was it so easy to be around her?

"Okay, so what is wrong with the patient?"

"Do you know how to perform a surgical cricothyrotomy?"

"Yes. I have done one before, but not when the patient is buried in a snowdrift."

"Peel off your mitts, because you're about to do one

on this mannequin. It's better to perfect it here in this simulation rather than on someone who is actually buried under snow." He tossed her a cricothyrotomy kit. "I'll time you."

"Do you want me to go through the steps as I'm doing it?" she asked as she pulled off her mitts.

"If you want."

She peeled back the cover on the kit and began to work. "Damn, my fingers are already going numb. This is going to be more difficult than I thought."

"Which is why we're practicing out here."

Sarah nodded. "Cricothyroid membrane detected and trachea grasped. Making incision."

Luke squatted down and watched her. "You're doing good."

She cursed under her breath. "My fingers are already numb."

"I know, but you can do it."

"Okay, making incision."

Luke watched as she made a beautiful incision in the skin. "Now expose the membrane with the handle of the scalpel."

"Got it." She set the scalpel down and finished the rest of the surgical cricothyrotomy. As she was suturing she cursed again. "My fingers are frozen."

"I know, but that's what happens."

Once it was finished, he handed her the mitts, which she hurriedly put on.

"You did a good job." Luke moved away from her quickly. "Well, I have to get ready and take those surveyors up the mountain. I'll see you later."

"Okay. Thanks." She scurried down off the snow pile and headed back inside. He didn't mind that. It was for the best, because she was stirring up things inside him that weren't welcome. Things that he'd thought were buried deep down.

He admired her. He had fun with her and he was highly attracted to her.

He wanted her and that was not good.

That was unacceptable.

CHAPTER SEVEN

AFTER THE TRAINING SESSION, Sarah had a shower and changed her clothes before heading into town. Her hands were still a little bit numb from performing that surgical cricothyrotomy out on the snow pile.

When she got to town she couldn't help but smile to see all the decorations going up. Hearts on the lampposts. Hearts in store windows. It was a small-town feel, like something straight from the movies, and it made her smile, even though she'd never felt so alone.

That was the thing about small towns. Everyone knew everyone. Or at least it seemed that way. Sarah was a stranger. All she knew was Luke and a couple people up at the hotel, but were they really her friends?

None of them were here with her. Really, she had no friends and it had never really bothered her before. She'd spent so many years distancing herself from her parents' world, she'd put up a wall to keep out everyone.

It hadn't bothered her until now. Even then she didn't know what she wanted. She wasn't sure that she could bring down those walls that were safe.

That were comfortable.

Sarah headed into the coffee shop that was on the corner of the main street. She was still shivering from the cold. When she entered the coffee shop, a few people stopped their conversation and looked in her direction, but only briefly. Being new in town generated some interest, but not enough for someone to come up and talk to her. And Sarah wasn't the kind to go up and start up a conversation with a stranger either.

If they were in a hospital or her clinic, then it would be no problem. She'd be able to talk to them quite easily.

Here, not a chance.

She made her way to the counter and sat down. It was like something out of the fifties. The coffee shop was a mishmash of retro and bohemian, but as long as they served good coffee she didn't care too much.

"What'll you have?" the girl behind the counter asked.

"A large black coffee with a shot of espresso, please."

"Will do." The girl moved away and Sarah undid her jacket and glanced around at all the people chatting. She envied them a bit.

"You're the new doctor in town, aren't you?"

Sarah turned to see a short, blonde woman slip into the seat next to her. It shocked her. In Manhattan this would've never happened. People she encountered in coffee shops there were always in a rush or kept to themselves, just as she did.

"I am," Sarah said. "I'm Dr. Ledet."

"I know." She grinned, her blue eyes twinkling. "I'm Dr. Esme Petersen."

"You're the cardio-thoracic surgeon."

Esme nodded. "I am. Luke mentioned that there was a new doctor up at the hotel. He also mentioned that you briefly worked with Dr. Eli Draven."

"I did. Do you know Dr. Draven?"

Esme nodded. "He trained me."

"I'm impressed. Dr. Draven is a world-class surgeon. Wait, Dr. Petersen, weren't you the one who inserted that chest tube into Shane Draven last summer?"

"I was," Esme said. "How did you know about that?"

"I was the surgeon in Missoula that operated on him."

Esme frowned slightly. "I thought you were from New York?"

"I was training some surgeons on a new technique when I was asked to help with incoming."

"What will you have, Dr. Petersen?" the girl asked as she set down Sarah's coffee in front of her.

"Cappuccino, please, Mary. Thanks."

"Sure thing." Mary walked away again.

"How are you enjoying Crater Lake?" Esme asked.

"It's been great." Sarah took a sip of her coffee. "It's quiet, though."

"Oh, no," Esme said. "You didn't just say that, did you?"

"What?"

"Quiet. I thought you were a trauma surgeon?" Esme said teasingly.

Sarah laughed. "How do you know so much about me?"

"It's a small town and you're new and shiny." Esme winked. "I was new and shiny last summer. I remember clearly."

Mary set down the cappuccino in front of Esme and disappeared again. Sarah could see that a heart was made in the foam.

"Aww, that's sweet," Sarah remarked.

Esme made a face. "I don't like Valentine's Day."

"What? I thought a heart surgeon would love Valentine's Day."

Esme took a swizzle stick and stabbed at the foam heart. "You'd think that, right?"

Sarah laughed. "You're the second person I've met in this town that hates Valentine's Day."

"Really? Who is the other person? Perhaps I should befriend them."

"Dr. Luke Ralston."

Esme laughed. "Luke? Oh, yeah, I forgot. He's such a grouch. I'm surprised he's talking to you, though."

"Why is that?"

"Well, he had a serious hate on for the surgeon who argued with him in Missoula."

Sarah started to laugh. "Yes. We didn't exactly get off on the right foot and I think I've been a thorn in his side."

"That doesn't surprise me. Although, it could work both ways. I think he might be a thorn in your side, too. He is in mine."

"Is he?"

"I'm dating Luke's brother, Carson. So, yeah, he's a bit of a pain in my butt."

"Has he ever dragged you out in the woods and forced you to train for emergency situations in minus-forty weather?" Sarah asked.

"Oh, he made you do that? What a jerk."

They both laughed at that. It was nice to chat with someone. It was nice to talk to someone and feel as if it wasn't superficial. She'd never had an easy chat with another woman before and certainly not another surgeon. She was used to being one of many sharks in a shark pond.

Once the coffee was done, Esme insisted on paying for both and they walked back out into the cold together and stood on the street.

"Thanks for having coffee with me. I was feeling a bit isolated up there," Sarah said.

Esme nodded and wound her knitted infinity scarf around, making a pretty knot in it. "I get it. I was once the new kid in town. Some people around here don't really like change. A few resent the resort community up there and the fact that there are a couple more that will be built, but most are coming around to the idea. It brings more business."

"How do you feel about a fourth doctor in town?" Sarah asked. "Is your practice suffering or is the other Dr. Ralston's?"

"No. It's steady. I get a lot of people from the outlying towns as I'm the closest cardio doctor. Were you worried?"

"Yeah, I didn't want to see an old family practice collapse."

"It won't." Esme reached out and squeezed her arm. "We should have coffee again or maybe even dinner. Carson's not a bad cook. Maybe we can even convince Luke to come down off that mountain."

Blood heated her cheeks and Sarah shook her head. "I seriously doubt that. He's up there now gallivanting around with surveyors."

Esme smiled. "Well, we'd still like to have you over sometime. Have a good day. Watch out for falling hearts."

"What?"

Esme pointed to the lamppost. "They tend to fall in a strong wind. It happened at Christmas. A Santa landed butt-first on a woman. It wasn't pretty."

Sarah nodded. "Thanks."

Esme walked down Main Street toward the clinic. Sarah glanced up at the glittery, tinsel hearts that were hanging off the lampposts. It made her smile. She jammed her hands in her pockets and headed back to her truck, but as she was walking back to the parking lot there was a rumble. A deep hollow sound followed by a large crack, like thunder, and then a roar like a jet plane was flying overhead. Sarah spun around and watched in horror as a cloud of snow spiraled up into the sky and moved like a wave down the side of the mountain.

It was an avalanche. She could hear screams from other residents of the town as the avalanche wiped away everything in its path.

It was close to home. It was large and it made Sarah's heart stop in her throat.

At least it was on the peak opposite the hotel. The peak was a remote site that could potentially be another hotel.

Then it hit her. That was the Lakeview trail that she'd been on only a couple of days ago. It was the trail that Luke was planning to take a group of surveyors up to.

Luke.

He was up there somewhere on that mountain and could be trapped.

Esme came rushing back up behind her. "Oh, my God. We have to get up that mountain."

"I drove the hotel's truck down."

Esme nodded. "Come help me grab supplies. Carson is already on his way from our place, but we need to get up there and see if anyone's been injured. Do you know where Luke is?"

"He was up there." Sarah pointed at the peak. "He was with surveyors."

Esme cursed under her breath. "I'm sure he's fine. He knows the danger signs. He wouldn't take them somewhere unsafe. Come on."

Sarah nodded, but she felt numb.

As if this weren't happening.

They just did a practice run of an avalanche emergency and now one had actually happened? She'd thought that Crater Lake would be a little bit more laid-back, but a bear mauling, a birth and now an avalanche? This place was just as busy as any city.

And last summer there was a landslide?

She'd thought living in the mountains would be peaceful, but she was beginning to realize just how isolated and dangerous it could be and she prayed that Luke had had the sense to see that taking the surveyors up on the Lakeview trail was dangerous and that he'd got out of the way of the avalanche.

"Luke, you're okay?"

Luke turned around to see his brother approaching the hotel. He was out of breath, as if he'd been running.

"I'm fine," Luke said.

Carson nodded and gave him a hug. "When I heard that crack I feared the worst. I knew you were going out on the trails today."

Luke nodded. "I saw the break in the cap before I set out. So I kept the surveyors at bay. I really thought, though, for a while that it wouldn't go and that they would be ticked off at me for wasting their time."

"Was anyone else on the mountain?" Carson asked.

"No. I shut the trails down to everyone else until that bear was caught. The game warden hadn't given me the okay to reopen them since the bear was subdued. We've had some mild temperatures at night and I knew we were due for an avalanche. I'm glad it was contained somewhat, though I'm still waiting to see how far it reached. There are some remote cabins in the way. I'm hoping it didn't get as far as Nestor's place."

Carson nodded. “Me, too. I’m glad you’re okay.”

Luke was going to say something further when he saw the resort truck driven by Sarah pull up and in the passenger side he saw Esme.

Great. Just great.

“Who’s that with Esme?”

“Dr. Ledet,” Luke mumbled.

Carson grinned. “No wonder I haven’t seen you for a while. I thought you were spending too much time up at the hotel.”

“What’s that supposed to mean?” Luke asked, glaring at his brother.

Carson nodded in Sarah’s direction. “I’ve seen her. I’m not blind. Isn’t that similar to what you said to me in the summer when Esme came to town?”

“Ha-ha. Your witty humor amuses me.”

Carson laughed out loud. “This explains a lot.”

“It explains nothing,” Luke snapped. “And you better remember that. I do have a large hank of rope in my truck. I still know how to set snares that entangle animals bigger than you.”

“Dad said you weren’t allowed to snare me anymore, remember?”

“No. I don’t.” Luke turned his back on his brother, giving Carson the hint he was done with this conversation and not to push him further. He looked back as Carson headed toward the truck to greet Esme and tell her that no one was hurt. Esme looked relieved and Carson kissed her.

Darn him.

Just for a moment Luke was jealous that his brother had that. Then he saw Sarah with a knapsack walking through the snow toward him and he smiled. She had a knapsack with her. She was learning and it made his heart melt, just a bit.

Don't let her in.

"I thought you were in town?" Luke asked gruffly as she set her bag down on the roof of Carson's truck.

"I was and then an avalanche hit. Was anyone hurt?"

"No. You are safe from performing any surgical cricothyrotomies for the moment."

She smiled. "That's great news. It looked so large I thought for sure someone was going to end up injured or worse."

"That actually wasn't too big. That was a medium."

Her eyes widened. "You're joking, right?"

"I don't joke."

"Right. I forgot. You're Mr. Serious all the time."

Luke grinned. "How did you know to bring up Dr. Petersen? I didn't know you knew each other."

"I didn't know her until today. We had coffee together."

Luke's stomach twisted. *Crap.* "What did you two talk about?"

"Wouldn't you like to know?" Her smile stretched from ear to ear.

Oh, Lord.

"Dr. Ralston?"

Luke turned to see one of the rangers coming toward him. "What's wrong, Officer Kyc?"

"The avalanche's zone has extended past Nestor's place. You're the most trained individual to go out and get him. If he was ten years younger and not suffering from cancer he'd be fine up there on his own, but…"

Luke nodded. "I'll get my gear together and go get him."

"Thanks, Dr. Ralston."

"Who's Nestor?" Sarah asked.

"He's a hermit. He likes to keep to himself. He really lives off the grid, taught me everything I know about surviving on the mountain. As much as the army did, but he's getting on in age and I'm not going to leave him up there to die."

"I'll go with you."

"Are you crazy?"

Sarah glared at him. "He might be injured. How are you going to get him down yourself?"

She had a point.

Carson wasn't equipped at the moment to go with him to get Nestor. It would take him over half an hour to get back home and change. There wasn't time. Luke wanted to get to Nestor before nightfall.

"Fine. Hurry up and get changed."

Sarah nodded and headed into the hotel. Luke scrubbed a hand over his face. What was he getting into?

She's just going to help me. Nestor needs help.

That was all there was to it. They were doing their job. That was it. They would go up and get Nestor and bring him back down to the hotel until they could clear a safe path for him to get to and from town. Luke had been giving him heck since the snow started to fly that he should move to town because of his cancer treatments, but Nestor wouldn't leave the mountain.

And really he couldn't blame him.

The mountain might be a harsh, cold and hard mistress, but she stood the test of time. She was more reliable than a heart.

CHAPTER EIGHT

THE SNOWSHOE WALK up to Nestor's cabin was brutal. Sarah knew it was going to be a long haul, but she really didn't have any idea until they were trudging through the snow, roped together for protection. Just in case one of them was swept away.

It terrified her, but she wouldn't back down.

She could do this. She was doing this.

At least Luke didn't treat her as if she were incapable of helping. In fact, he was the first person in a long time who actually appreciated her help. Instead of doing stuff for her, he taught her how. He pushed her to her limits. Made her work and feel things that she'd thought were buried deep inside her.

She hadn't thought that he would let her, to be honest. She knew that he was wary about letting her accompany him, she could see that plainly on his face, but one thing she'd learned about Luke Ralston was he wasn't an idiot.

Sarah knew, just as much as he did, that it would be faster for her to get suited up and assist him than it would for his brother, Carson. She knew that she would be traversing into dangerous territory, but a life was at stake.

She wasn't going to pass up on that. That wasn't the kind of doctor she was.

So without complaint she'd strapped on the heavy rucksack laden with supplies, strapped on the snowshoes and had let Carson tie a rope between Luke and her. It was a lifeline, just in case she slipped and fell. Or just in case the snowcap decided it would crack again and sweep them away.

When she finally saw the cabin in a small clearing she let out an inward sigh of relief at the sight of it and she quickened her pace to keep up with Luke.

Luke stopped in a small copse of trees and set down his rucksack, but he didn't make a move to untie it.

"Why are we stopping?" Sarah asked, though secretly she was glad. She was in pretty good shape, but she wasn't used to the strenuous pace that Luke had kept, or to how much of a sweat she'd worked up under all her winter gear.

"We need a break. Just five minutes to catch our breath and have some water. You okay with that?"

"Perfectly." Sarah dropped her backpack next to Luke's and pulled out her canteen, taking a big swig of water.

"I'm impressed you brought a backpack," he said.

"Of course. I wouldn't have heard the end of it if I hadn't."

He chuckled. "This is true."

"So, if this Nestor guy is a hermit how do you know him? Don't hermits usually keep to themselves?"

"*Hermit* is probably the wrong word. Nestor just likes to live off the land. He's a pioneer man."

"And how do you know him?"

"He taught me everything I know about survival. I could make up a brilliant story about how he saved my life, or something, but really it was just because my father and he were friends. I always took a real interest in what he had to say. He's like a second father to me. Since my dad moved away and my brother, Carson, started dating Dr. Petersen I've been hanging around Nestor quite a bit." Luke smiled. "He's the only one who ever believed in me when I went to the army."

"Your father didn't approve?"

Luke snorted. "Not really. He wanted me to go to the same medical school as my brother and then to train in the same hospital. My father wanted Carson and I to be partners, but that's not what I wanted. I never wanted that." Luke frowned. "Anyway, Nestor was the only one who told me to follow my dreams."

Sarah was a bit taken aback. It was the first time Luke had ever really talked, opening up warmly about someone else. She'd thought he kept everyone out. That he was cold and closed-off. But underneath that hard surface there was something more about him.

Something warm and loving.

"Is he the one who taught you how to build a log cabin?"

Luke grinned. "He is. He helped me quite a bit. He would like me to live more off the grid, but I do like some modern conveniences."

"Are you sure about that, Pa?" Sarah teased. "You did make all your furniture."

"Yeah, but I like electricity and running water too much." Luke stood up. "We'd better get going. Night falls fast, and we don't want to be trying to bring Nestor down off the mountain in the dark."

Sarah nodded. "Okay."

They packed their canteens back in their bags and headed out on their journey again. Now she understood why Luke was so concerned about getting up there to see if Nestor was okay. It wasn't just the first responder training in him. Luke *cared* about Nestor.

He was worried, and she couldn't even begin to imagine what he must be feeling.

Can't you?

Then she remembered how panicked she'd been when the avalanche had first hit and she'd thought Luke was up there in its path. That was probably nothing compared to worrying about someone who meant something to you.

Luke means something to you, though, doesn't he?

Sarah shook that thought away. There was no time to think about things like that. She had to stay focused on the task at hand. She wouldn't be the one to slow Luke down from getting to his friend in an emergency situation.

When they were at the house, they dropped their knapsacks, undid the rope and took off their snowshoes, propping them inside the lean-to.

"If you think I'm rustic, Nestor is worse," Luke said, kicking the snow off his boots. Then he pounded on the door. "Nestor, it's Ralston. There's been an avalanche."

There was no response.

Luke knocked again. "Nestor, open up."

"It's awfully dark in there and there's no smoke coming from the chimney," Sarah said.

Luke grinned. "I'm impressed you noticed that. Most people from the city don't think about a chimney or smoke from a fire. I'm going to check in the back window."

Sarah nodded while Luke put his snowshoes back on and walked to the back of the house. Sarah stood there waiting. The only sound was her breaths. There was no wind howling in the natural wind break where Nestor's cabin was nestled. There were no birds, no rustling of evergreen needles. It was deadly calm, like right before a storm.

It was a nice spot, but as she glanced through the forest she could see a wall of snow from where the avalanche had barely missed his cabin. It was at least six feet high, with broken and snapped trees everywhere.

She shuddered. It was eerie. Something was not right. She didn't know what, but she could feel it in her bones that something was wrong.

"He's gone," Luke said as he came back into the lean-to.

"You mean he's dead?"

"No, I mean there was a note that he got down before the avalanche hit. He left for Missoula two days ago for his chemo treatment."

"For a hermit who lives off the grid on the side of the mountain I'm surprised he's undertaking chemo."

Luke chuckled. "Well, that might be my doing and his son's, too. Greg came up here last summer and gave his father a stern talking-to. He tried to convince him to move to Missoula with him permanently, but he refused. They struck this bargain. Well, the rangers will be glad to hear that he's not in harm's way. Though I wish he'd checked in with them or me at least."

"So we can head back to the hotel?"

He nodded. "Yep. Sorry, I know you're a bit bushed. Though I'm glad you came, and I'm glad you came prepared and were able to keep up with me. I know I move faster on snowshoes than you're used to."

"It's no problem. I had a good teacher."

Luke's easygoing smile disappeared. "Yes...well, I'm

glad you came. Had he been injured, two sets of medically trained hands would have been better than one. Especially when both sets are trained in trauma."

She had obviously made him uncomfortable, which had not been her intention. She'd meant every word she'd said about him being a good teacher. A month ago she wouldn't have had a clue what to do.

She shrugged. "It's no big deal. I'm just glad he's not injured and we don't have to drag him back down."

"Me, too. Let's go before it gets too dark."

Sarah nodded and put on her snowshoes and slung on her knapsack. Luke led the way out of the lean-to and retied the rope between them. That was when she noticed that it was getting dark. Fast. The clouds were low, thick and full of snow. She might not be native to Montana, but, after living in New York and now here, she could recognize snow clouds.

"Do you think a storm is coming?" she asked when they were through the trees back out into the clearing, following the same path they'd taken before.

Luke stopped and looked around. "Yeah, I think so, but we'll beat it."

"You sure?"

"Positive, but we..." He trailed off as he looked up the slope. She looked where he was looking and saw a crack, spreading across a huge chunk of snow.

Oh, my God.

The horror dawned on her fast, because they were right in its path.

"Throw your pack and kick off your snowshoes. Now!" Luke shouted.

Sarah's pulse thundered in her ears and she heaved her knapsack as far as she could, before kicking off her snowshoes. She sank into the deep snow as a loud crack thundered across the slope. The rumbling struck dread in her, right down to her very core, as she tried to run back to the cabin. If the cabin was buried, at least it would be some kind of shelter. Nestor had been smart and built it into the slope, but running through the snow toward salvation was like trying to move through deep sand. It was heavy and it felt as if her limbs weighed a hundred pounds.

"Remember to swim, Sarah. Swim!"

Luke was close to her. All Sarah wanted to do was cling to him, but survival instincts kicked in and as that wave of snow hit she used her arms to swim, fighting the current of snow that tried to drive her down the mountain. Her body screamed in agony as she swam, the rope between Luke and her taut. She didn't even know if he was still there.

All she had to do was keep swimming. She had to keep her head above the snow. She had to breathe.

There was a yank on her arm and she was pulled out of the torrent of snow and fell on top of Luke, who was gasping for breath. One arm tightened around her as the snow roared and thundered past them.

She buried her face in his chest and tried not to cry. She just clung to him. He was her lifeline in this moment. When the roar stopped, only then did she lift her head up and see that their path was cut off and the snow swirling around them was a storm just getting started.

She didn't know how long they had been fighting the avalanche. It felt like hours the way her body ached. Snow had crept through every crack of her snowsuit.

"You okay?" Luke asked. There was a deep cut to his forehead, by his hairline. It was bleeding profusely.

"I'm fine," she whispered and then she got off him and stood up, her legs weak and her head spinning. "You're bleeding."

"It's a scalp laceration. I'm okay. We need to get to shelter." Luke got up and winced. "At least we have Nestor's place."

Sarah saw that they had been pushed farther down quite a bit, but at least Nestor's cabin had only been partially buried. The lean-to was uncovered and they had access to the door. It was a way inside.

"Come on," Luke said. "We'll get inside and start a fire. Once the storm dies down, they'll send for help."

Sarah nodded and then she spied the backpacks a few feet down at the edge of the pile. "Look, the backpacks made it."

"Good. The snowshoes didn't. I'll break the path. You follow."

Sarah stayed close behind Luke as he broke a path down to the backpacks. Her legs were like jelly, but the storm was getting worse and they had to seek shelter. Once they retrieved their backpacks they headed up to Nestor's cabin.

Luke managed to force the door and they were out of the wind. It was cold in the cabin, but Sarah didn't care. At least they were safe in here. It was shelter.

"Can you tape some gauze to my lac?" Luke asked.

"You'll need more than a dressing. You'll need stitches."

"I know, but first you'll need some boiling water to clean it out and sterilize and to do that I need to start a fire. It's hard to operate with blood dripping in my eye."

"Sure." Sarah pulled out the first-aid kit and did a quick patchwork on Luke's laceration. Then she helped him bring in a lot of wood. While he started the fire in the fireplace, she grabbed a large pot and filled it with snow from outside the lean-to so they could boil it. Nestor had an old-fashioned water pump, but it was frozen.

It didn't take Luke long to get a fire started, which began to heat up the small cabin in no time. Sarah pulled out their sleeping bags from the bottom of their knapsacks.

"Zip them together," Luke said, wincing slightly.

"What?" she asked.

"Body heat in the night. Nestor only has one small bunk over there. We won't both fit and he's shorter than I am. I know I won't fit on that bunk."

Sarah nodded and zipped the bags together. "I should really take a look at that laceration. Get it cleaned and stitched up. The blood is soaking through the gauze."

Luke agreed, his face pale as he sat down in front of the fire. Sarah found an oil lamp and lit it so she could see a little bit better. She carefully peeled off the bandage and inspected the wound and his head.

"I don't feel a fracture."

"I know," he said. "It's just a laceration. I'm fine."

Sarah glared at him. "Don't play brave with me. It's a deep lac. I'm the one with the needle. I'm sorry I don't have any anesthetic. I do have some morphine for after, though."

He shook his head. "It's okay. I'm not playing brave. I've been stitched up before like this. Just do it."

"Okay. At least it won't need a lot of stitches."

He didn't say much, just looked off into the distance over her shoulder as she got ready to suture. There were a few winces, but mostly he didn't make a peep as she threw four stitches into his forehead, disinfected and then bandaged up the wound. She threw the bloody gauze into the fire and then used the antibacterial foam to clean her hands.

Luke got up and started rummaging around in Nestor's cupboards.

"What're you looking for?" she asked.

"Something to numb the pain," he said.

"I have morphine."

"Ah ha!" Luke pulled out a bottle of amber liquid. "Whiskey. Much better than morphine."

She laughed. "Much better, but won't Nestor be angry that we're rifling through his cupboards?"

"Nah, he'll know this is an emergency. I'll replace everything we have to use."

Sarah began to shiver again. "I think my socks are wet."

"Mine, too. We have to get out of these damp, cold clothes and into the sleeping bag to preserve body heat."

What?

Only she couldn't say that out loud, because her mouth dropped open and she felt a bit dumbstruck at the moment.

Luke moved past her and started to strip off his outer gear and then took off his flannel shirt, exposing his chest and back. Sarah didn't need a fire at that moment, because she realized that he was expecting her to climb naked into a double sleeping bag with him.

"I can't get naked."

He glanced around, hanging up his clothes. The only thing on him was his trousers and she couldn't help but notice how incredibly ripped and tanned Luke was under all those flannel shirts he wore. Her body was very aware that she was going to see all of him in a matter of moments and that he would see her.

She'd never undressed in front of a man before.

The last time she made love to a man, she didn't undress in front of him. It was done in dignity with the lights out and, even then, she really couldn't remember much about that encounter because, like the rest of her past romantic life, it hadn't been overly memorable.

Who says you're going to have sex?

The cabin was heating up and it wasn't just the fire.

"What's wrong? Why can't you get undressed?"

She crossed her arms. "I don't get naked in front of strange men."

"I'm not a stranger. Besides, if you don't you'll most likely get hypothermia. Okay, I'll close my eyes until you get into the sleeping bag. I swear to you, nothing untoward will happen."

"What about the extra clothes in the knapsack?" she asked. "You told me to always pack extra clothes."

"They'll be too cold and we've been exposed outside too long. This is the fastest way to get our temperature back up. Besides, we're doctors. It's not like we haven't seen naked bodies before."

Dammit.

He had a point. The only difference was, she hadn't seen him naked before and vice versa. There was a difference between seeing a patient for an exam and seeing a man you were highly attracted to, naked.

"Okay." She began to peel off her clothes and hung them near the fire so they could dry and just as she did that Luke peeled off his pants and her breath caught in her throat at the sight of his very muscular, well-defined backside.

She tried not to look, because she didn't want him to see the blush that she knew was slowly creeping up her neck into her cheeks.

This was going to be a very long night.

CHAPTER NINE

LUKE WAS TRYING very hard to ignore the fact that in a few moments he was going to be inches away from Sarah and that she was going to be naked. He'd fantasized about having her naked in his bed before, but this was not how he'd pictured it.

When he glanced over at her, her pale cheeks were flaming red and she was looking away. He felt bad for her, so he walked across the room to Nestor's bed and wrapped a blanket around his waist. Then grabbed another quilt and walked back over to her.

"I'm respectable."

She opened her eyes and he held out the blanket. "Where did you get these?"

"Nestor's bed. Besides, the extra blankets will help keep us warm."

She nodded. "Thanks."

He moved away from her and tried not to look at her as he climbed into the sleeping bag. He poured himself a shot of whiskey and swigged it down quickly, trying to numb the pain of his throbbing head and also to try and distract himself from the fact that Sarah was undressing a few feet away from him.

How many times had he thought about this? Too many

times. His pulse was racing, his blood had heated and he was fighting to control his yearning for her.

The only trouble was being in Sarah's presencc did that to him.

When he was in her presence he lost all control.

He wished he could just take her in his arms and make love to her like he desperately wanted to.

Don't think about it.

Only he couldn't help it and he stifled a groan.

"You okay?" she asked as she wrapped the blanket around her and then climbed into the sleeping bag beside him.

"My head hurts, just a bit." He didn't want to admit to her that the groan he'd been trying to get under control had nothing to do with the injury to his head.

"Well, that's to be expected. I can get the morphine."

"Stop pushing drugs on me." He winked at her and she laughed, but she still seemed nervous.

She's not the only one.

"Fine. Have another shot of whiskey, then."

"I will," Luke said and he poured her a cup, handing it to her. "First you. It'll warm you up."

"Thanks." She took a sip. "That does help."

He nodded. "I told you it would. You did really good out there today."

"You taught me well." She took another sip of whiskey. "You told me to swim and I did, but that..."

"I know. When that avalanche hit us and I started to swim, it was powerful. More powerful than any current I've swam in, in water. Being in that avalanche was like nothing I've ever felt before. I'm glad we weren't swept away down the side of the mountain. It was a minor one."

"That was minor? I thought you'd experienced an avalanche before?"

"I've seen them, I've helped those injured, but never have I experienced almost being swept away by one."

"At least we weren't trapped." Sarah shivered; he could hear her teeth chattering. So he moved closer, wrapping his arm around her. His blood pounding between his ears, because he was touching her.

You're just keeping her warm. That's all.

Her breath hitched in her throat the moment he pulled her close. Her skin was so soft, the flowery scent of her silken, blond hair surrounding him and he wanted to pull it out of the braid she'd put it in and run his fingers through it.

"No, we weren't trapped. That's a good thing." Only right now in this cabin they were trapped by the storm. Being here with her, with nothing between them, was more dangerous to him than being trapped in that snowstorm.

He was nervous, but he couldn't pull himself away.

You're just warming her, he told himself again.

"That feels good," she whispered.

"What does?" he asked.

"Your arm around me." Then she moved in closer to him and touched his face. Her fingers lightly brushing over his skin, which made him feel as if he were on fire. Her lips so close to his. Then her fingers touched his lips and he closed his eyes, trying to regain control of his senses, but before he could maintain that control, before he could stop what was happening her lips pressed against his in a feather-light kiss. He tried not to cup her face and drag her tight against his body, as he wanted to. He'd forgotten what a woman's kiss felt like.

He'd forgotten what passion tasted like. It had been far too long and he was caught off guard by it. It rocked him to his very core and he didn't want it to end. He wanted more.

Oh, God.

Luke needed to put an end to this before he got carried away and forgot himself. Before he forgot why he distanced himself from women, about why he distanced himself from her.

"Why did you do that?" he asked.

"I wanted to. I've wanted to for some time." Her blue eyes sparkled in the dim flickering light thrown from the fire. "I want to kiss you again, Luke."

"I don't think that's wise," he said, though his body screamed yes, yes, yes.

"I don't think it's particularly wise either," she whispered, but then her hands ran through his hair and she was kissing him urgently.

He should push her away, but the moment she sighed and melted against him he was a lost man.

He was completely lost to her.

Luke undid the braid in her hair and gently ran his fingers through it. It was as soft as he'd imagined. Like silk. It fanned over her bare shoulder and he couldn't help but brush it away. Ever since he'd first met her, he'd dreamed of touching her skin, her hair, and now he was.

He'd forgotten what it was like.

Christine had hurt him so bad with her betrayal and he'd buried these feelings deep inside. He didn't ever want to feel like that again, but in this moment he was reveling in being with Sarah and he was worried that if he indulged then he wouldn't ever be able to stop.

That he'd want more.

And he couldn't have more.

He wouldn't put his heart at risk again. When Christine left him, he'd promised himself he wouldn't let another woman affect him like that. Love just brought pain.

Who said anything about love?

He moved away. He couldn't do this even though he desperately wanted to.

"What's wrong?" Sarah asked.

"I don't know if we should be doing this."

"Doing what?" she asked.

"Kissing."

"I think we should be." Sarah touched his face again and then kissed him. "I don't think we should stop."

"Sarah, I can't promise you anything."

She smiled at him. "I'm not asking for promises. I just want you. Here and now."

"I want you, too. I can't help myself, but I do."

And it was true. When it came to Sarah, he couldn't help himself.

Sarah wasn't sure what made her reach out and kiss Luke. It wasn't the whiskey, that was for certain. She could hold her drink better than most. No, she was sure it was due to the fact that moments ago she'd almost died.

Working in the ER Sarah had seen countless people face death, sometimes because of the simplest reasons, like a reaction to a medication or food and sometimes because of something more complicated that damaged their body. She'd wrestled with death in the OR, saving patients while she operated on them and, though they could never remember that moment when they came so close to losing the battle because they'd been under general anesthesia, she always wondered what it might be like.

Did they feel anything?

Did they see their life flash before their eyes, even in a dreamless sleep?

Did they understand how close they came and how hard they fought, how hard she fought for them? Overcoming death for her patients was a high. The lives she saved meant more to her than all the money her parents had.

It was why she did what she did.

So when her moment came it was surreal. When the snow came roaring down the hill toward her, there was a clarity.

Live or die.

And she chose life. She fought hard. She swam and when she came through it, it hit her how many chances she'd passed on. Not when it came to her career, but her life. She'd been fighting her whole life to prove to her parents she was her own person, to the point that she didn't know when to stop fighting. Maybe life didn't always have to be such a fight? Maybe she hadn't really been living her life, because she was so busy trying to show everyone that she was capable of doing things on her own that life was passing her by. She wasn't even sure anymore.

When she thought she had been living her own life, she hadn't. Her father had made that painfully clear. She'd spent so long building up walls that now she wanted Luke on the other side with her.

She wanted to live her life. Take chances, take risks, because even though that avalanche had been the most terrifying thing she'd ever experienced, surviving after the fact was equally scary.

Right now, in this moment with Luke, she just wanted to feel. She chose this and she wanted it.

Really she shouldn't but she couldn't fight it anymore. She wanted Luke as she'd never wanted another man before. It was something fierce. Primal, even. It scared her and thrilled her.

She wanted to feel again.

"Sarah, I'll ask again. Are you sure?"

"I'm sure."

Luke rolled over, pressing her against the floor and laying kisses against her lips, her neck and lower. He brushed his knuckles down the side of her face and kissed where her pulse raced under her skin.

"You make me feel," he whispered. Then he leaned down and brushed another kiss against her lips, light and then urgent. His body was pressed against hers. It made her feel right and she loosened the extra blanket he'd given her so they could be skin to skin. She opened her legs to let him settle between her thighs. Sarah arched her hips. She wanted him.

She craved him.

"I have to stop," Luke moaned.

"Why?"

"I don't have protection. One thing I didn't pack for."

Sarah grinned. "It's okay. I'm on birth control and I'm clean."

"So am I. Are you sure you want to, though?"

"Yes. I want to. The question is do you want me?" She bucked her hips and he groaned.

"Oh, I want you."

"How much?"

Luke kissed her again, his tongue pushing past her

lips, entwining with hers, showing her just how much he wanted her.

"I want you so much." He ran his hands over her body, his hands hot, branding her skin as he touched her.

"I've tried hard to resist you," Sarah whispered against his neck. "You drive me crazy."

He grinned. "I want you, too, Sarah."

Luke's lips captured hers in a kiss, silencing any more words between them. Sarah pulled him closer and wrapped her legs against his waist. His hands slipped down her sides.

"So beautiful," he murmured.

His hand slid between them and he began to stroke her. Sarah bit her lip to stop from crying out. She wanted so much more. She wanted Luke inside her. She wanted him to take her and make her feel again.

Sarah wanted Luke to remind her of who she was, because she couldn't remember. She just wanted to forget it all and get lost in this one moment with him.

"I love having you under me," Luke whispered against her neck. "I want to be inside you."

"I want you, too."

He pushed her down, covering her body with his and thrusting into her. Sarah cried out then. She couldn't help herself. Being joined with him was overwhelming, but it was what she wanted. It was what she needed.

"You feel so good," he moaned. "Damn."

She moved her hips, urging him to move, but he wouldn't. He just held her still, buried deep inside her.

"You're evil," she gasped.

"I know."

Luke moved slowly at first, taking his time, and it drove her crazy. She wanted him hard and fast. She wanted to feel him moving inside her. She urged him to go faster until he lost all control and was thrusting against her hard and fast. Then she could feel her body succumbing to the sweet release she was searching for. Pleasure overtook her and she cried out again, digging her nails into his back, making him hiss in pain, but it didn't stop him. He kept going until his own release came a moment later.

He rolled away onto his back and she curled up on his chest, just listening to his heart race. It was soothing and reassuring. She'd always liked the sound of the heart. It meant life. Then tears started to roll down her face.

"Sarah, are you okay?"

She sat up, trying to brush the tears away. "I'm fine."

"Do you regret what happened?"

"No," she said quickly. "No. I wanted that to happen. What happened here tonight was a long time coming. It's just…we could've died today."

He smiled softly. "But we didn't."

"I know. You know, it was in that moment on the slope that I couldn't recall if the life I've been living has been my own."

Luke's brow furrowed. "How do you mean?"

"Everything I've accomplished is because my father has had a hand in it."

"What?"

"You want to know why I came here? I came here because my father got my last job for me. Just like every other job. So I came here, without his help. I'm tired of being labelled as his helpless daughter."

Luke nodded. "Stepping out of a parent's shadow can be hard. And you're far from helpless."

Sarah sighed. "I'm not sure if I know myself anymore."

"I understand that."

She frowned. "Do you? You're living out your dream here."

Luke shrugged. "I love the mountains, but it wasn't my dream to be a lone wolf. I was married before."

"You were?"

He nodded. "She left me for my best friend while I was overseas."

"No wonder you have trust issues."

"Yeah. I suppose I do."

Luke turned from her, withdrawing from her once more. But for a moment she had seen a little piece of himself that he kept hidden from the world.

Sarah had been absolutely shocked to learn that he'd been married before. He just didn't seem the type to settle down with a wife, and she couldn't help but wonder what he'd been like before he'd become this walled-off man.

And no wonder, when his wife had left him for his best friend. Two people he'd trusted completely had betrayed him.

It explained so much, but Sarah had a feeling there was more to it than that. There was something else he wasn't saying.

"It's hard to trust when you trust no one."

Luke turned back around. "What?"

"At least you have a family to turn to. I don't. I can't rely on my parents."

"Why?"

"They were never around."

"I'm sorry."

Sarah shrugged. "My mother preferred the company of her friends over her children and my dad was too involved with his businesses. Money drives him."

"Must've been a lonely childhood."

She nodded. The words, though the truth, stung. Her whole life had been lonely up until now. She had just never realized it.

How could she trust a man who guarded his heart so? He'd never open up fully. His ex-wife had hurt him terribly, and in the short time Sarah had known him she'd learned that he didn't give people a second chance.

He was stubborn that way.

Which was a shame.

"It was. I sometimes felt invisible," she said. She hadn't intended to say that thought out loud, but she had.

He moved toward her and touched her face briefly "I get not knowing who you are anymore. I get it, but I want you to know. I see you."

She wanted to believe him. She really did, but she didn't think anyone could see her, especially when she couldn't even see herself. So long she'd been under her family's thumb, she didn't even know it. How could she believe him, when she couldn't even believe in herself?

"You don't believe me," Luke said.

"What?"

"Your expression. I can read you like a book."

She glared at him. "Thanks."

"It's something I've learned to do as an army medic."

"Why did you leave the army?"

His demeanor changed almost instantly. "What?"

"What made you change your mind about the army?"

"I thought I had a wife waiting for me."

"I'm sorry."

Luke shrugged and then unzipped his side of the sleeping bag. "Are you hungry?"

"Sure." She watched him as he dug in his knapsack

for his dry pair of pants and slipped them on. "Hey, I thought you said we shouldn't wear our extra clothes?"

He grinned. "That was when we were still damp and cold. I bet you're warm now."

She blushed and then grabbed her knapsack, pulling out the dry set of clothes and pulling on the pants, shirt and socks. There was a definite draught on the floor. She got up and padded toward the window. It was dark, but that was about all she knew. She couldn't see a thing. All she could hear was the howling from the wind.

"Still storming?" Luke asked as he pulled down some cans from Nestor's cupboard and set them down on the counter.

"It looks that way. How long do you think it will last?"

Luke shrugged. "I don't know. Probably not that long. Usually when a bad blizzard is about to whip up, they warn us. The only warning I heard for today was a squall."

"I think that's more than a squall out there."

Luke nodded. "Nestor has beans. I hope you don't mind."

"Yes. I totally mind." She walked over to him. "I don't think those hearts will survive."

"What?" he asked as she rifled through drawers.

"I was in town and they were decorating for Valentine's Day."

Luke snorted. "Of course. They're probably going overboard, too, because of the big party that's going to happen on Valentine's Day at the hotel. Just the idea of the town covered in all that paraphernalia makes me a bit queasy."

"Well, the resident party planners have been working

around the clock since I arrived in Crater Lake. I think it's going to be a big party."

Luke snorted again. "Pointless."

"Why?"

"Darn it, do you think Nestor could keep things in a logical spot?" Luke cursed again and bent down to rummage under the counter.

Sarah rolled her eyes. There was no getting through to him. At least not about this or why he left the army. His ex-wife really did a number on him and she felt bad that he'd been hurt. He'd been betrayed by the woman he loved and she'd been betrayed by her parents in a way.

Though really it wasn't the same thing.

They were both damaged souls and she hadn't made any promise to him, just as he had never made any to her. She didn't regret what had happened between them here tonight. She was glad it had happened.

Even if it could never happen again, because she couldn't let it happen again. Luke was her friend and she wouldn't hurt him the way his ex-wife had hurt him and she doubted very much Luke would even let her in if she tried.

His heart was guarded, just as much as she had her own walls of protection up. At least he'd let her in just briefly, even for a moment.

It was better they remained friends. Just friends and coworkers. That was all they could be, but that made her sad and for one brief moment she wished for something more.

CHAPTER TEN

AFTER THEY HAD something to eat they curled up together by the fire to spend the night and even though Luke wanted something to happen again, he wouldn't allow it. If it were warmer in Nestor's cabin he would've had her sleep on Nestor's bunk and he would've stayed on the floor.

Sarah fell asleep almost instantly after they had something to eat, but Luke couldn't sleep. Which ticked him off. If the storm subsided they were going to have to hike out of here. He knew that Nestor had snowshoes and skis in the lean-to, but in order to hike back down to the resort he would need his energy and that required sleep.

Especially after the strenuous activity that they'd engaged in a couple hours ago.

Don't think about it.

He didn't want to let Sarah in and risk his heart. The trouble was, she was already digging her way in there. He couldn't fall in love again. It was too much of a risk.

And living up on a mountain tracking bears and rescuing stranded people isn't?

What if Sarah decided to head back to New York? What if she wanted him to give up his life here and when he couldn't she'd leave him?

He wouldn't be hurt again. He wouldn't put his heart in that kind of danger again. It wasn't worth it. It was pointless.

Luke cursed under his breath and slowly climbed out of the sleeping bag, making sure that he didn't disturb Sarah. He wandered over to the window and peered outside. The snowstorm was beginning to subside. He could see black instead of just a wall of white.

He glanced back over at her, sleeping so peacefully, her blond hair fanned out around her head, and he desperately wanted to go back and join her. If he'd been in a different place.

If he'd never married Christine.

When Christine had left it hurt, but it also relieved him because he was beginning to see that they weren't meant for each other.

It was a clean break.

Still, it hurt. The betrayal stung.

Trust was not something he gave easily or freely.

So yeah, risking his life on the mountain was not playing it safe, but the only one who was affected by the choices he made was him. There was no wife to think about. No kids. He was free.

Really?

He sighed. Yeah, he was free, but the cost of his freedom was loneliness. He hadn't realized how lonely he had been until Sarah ended up in Crater Lake. When he'd started working with her, he'd been dreading it at first, because all he'd remembered was the surgeon from the summer. The one who'd rankled him and had fire in her eyes.

This Sarah was different from that surgeon from the summer.

She still was a spitfire, but something had changed in her.

The fire was diminished. He shouldn't really care why, but he did. And he discovered that he looked forward to all their training sessions. Although, she didn't know that those sessions weren't Silas Draven's idea, but his.

At first he was supposed to show her a bit of emergency first aid and tell her about some of the common injuries that could occur on the mountain, especially injuries that would happen to guests, but, after taking her out that first time and seeing how she threw herself into everything she did, he wanted to show her more.

And he soon found that he liked spending the time with her. Which was bad, because the more time he spent with her, the more his walls came down and he didn't like that.

Those walls were there for a reason. Those walls protected him.

Those walls would protect her.

He didn't want to stop being a first responder. He didn't want to stop doing what he was doing, because it mattered and because of that he wouldn't leave a widow or children behind. A life of solitude was the only answer.

It was the only way. That way no one got hurt.

I need to put some distance between us.

As soon as they were back at the resort, Luke was going to sever ties with Sarah for a while. She'd move on and find someone else. He had no doubt. She was beautiful, kind, funny. Of course, thinking about someone else kissing her made him angry.

She can't be yours.

And he had to keep reminding himself of that fact. The squalling stopped, almost as suddenly as it had started, which was good. He just hoped another system wasn't about to start up again. He didn't want to eat all of Nestor's rations.

Just as he was about to turn away, he saw lights coming up off the trail. Several lights and he realized they were snowmobiles.

"Sarah, wake up!" he shouted.

She bolted upright. "What's wrong?"

"Our rescue team has arrived."

She was confused. "What?"

"The squall ended and there's a pack of snowmobiles headed this way."

She got up and ran over to the window. "Oh, thank goodness. At least we don't have to hike down the mountain tomorrow. I'll start packing up."

Luke nodded and then grabbed his dry flannel shirt, quickly pulling it on as well as his socks and boots. If he didn't know any better, his brother or Esme would be on one of those snowmobiles and he wasn't going to have them catch him half-naked in a cabin with Sarah. He wasn't going to be subjected to their constant questioning for the next few weeks.

As soon as his boots were on there was a knock at the door.

"Luke?"

It was Carson. Luke opened the door and his brother let out a sigh of relief and pulled him into a bear hug.

"You're freezing and I just got warm. Get in here."

The rescue team shuffled into the small entrance way of Nestor's cabin. Carson and two other first responders had come up the mountain.

"We were about to call off the search," Carson said. "Then I saw smoke coming from Nestor's cabin. We found out about twenty minutes after you and Sarah left that Nestor was in Missoula with his family getting chemotherapy. And then the avalanche. I'm glad you're okay. I'm glad you're both okay."

"Yeah, we learned he was gone when we got here. We were heading back when the avalanche struck, but we got out of it."

"We swam," Sarah said.

Carson and the first responders looked at her in shock. "You swam? You mean you were hit by the avalanche?"

"Yeah, but it was minor. Then the squall hit, so we got back to Nestor's and broke in. I owe him some provisions and some firewood."

"I don't think he'll mind," Carson said. "We should get back down the mountain before another squall hits. Last check on radar was another one was brewing to the northwest of here."

Luke nodded. "We'll pack our things and get our gear on."

Carson and the other two men stepped outside into the lean-to.

Sarah was shoving the last of her things into her knapsack. The zipped-together bags were undone and the blankets had been folded and put back on Nestor's bed. It was as if what had happened between them had been swept away.

It's for the best.

"I'll be glad to get back to my own bed. Maybe even a hot shower," she remarked as she zipped up her coat.

"Yeah. Me, too." Which was a lie. Even though he knew it was for the best this was happening, deep down he secretly wished he could spend the night with her, but he shook that thought away as he finished packing his things and putting out the fire.

Sarah was already outside, by the time the fire had been extinguished and the oil lamp turned off. The cabin was so dark and lonely. The small window panes illuminated by the headlights from the snowmobiles.

He wished they could stay, just for a bit longer, but this was better.

Luke was getting the distance he needed from her.

And if he did that, he would have a chance for his walls to rebuild.

Yeah. Right.

It was the fastest ride she'd ever been on. One of the responders, named Lee, had said that there was another squall brewing and they were trying to beat it back to the resort.

Sarah didn't care at that moment. All she wanted to do was get back to her bed, electricity and a hot shower. She didn't want to be stuck in another squall, in a shack and eating beans. Although, the company was fine.

She didn't mind that in the least.

Luke was on the snowmobile with his brother and Sarah wished that he were driving one of the machines and that she were riding with him.

Something had changed up there and she didn't know what it was, other than he was more closed off than before. He barely looked her in the eye and it frightened her.

Who cares? You both were consenting adults and didn't make any promises.

Only, when it was all over with, she found herself craving more. She wanted him again, but that was not possible. If she took up with Luke, her mother would be somewhat happy that she'd found a doctor to settle down with, but then her father would say to her again that she couldn't handle the job in Crater Lake on her own.

You try too hard, pumpkin. You don't need to try so hard.

She hated when her father talked down to her like that. As if she were still four years old. She was the baby and therefore couldn't make it on her own.

As much as she wanted to be with Luke, maybe a little distance was a good thing. Besides, he wasn't telling her something. There was some hurt still buried there. How could she trust him if he couldn't trust her?

He didn't seem to take much stock in love. As was evident by his hatred for Valentine's Day and intimacy.

She didn't understand why he felt this way, other than his failed marriage, but there had to be something more to it than that. How could someone have so much hate for an emotion that also brought joy? Yeah, love did hurt, but in the end wasn't it worth it?

Of course, she wouldn't know anything about love.

She'd never been in it. She'd had crushes or relationships, but love? That was something she'd never experienced. It was scary and messy. She just didn't have time for it.

Why not?

She shook that thought from her head as the snowmobiles slowed down and came to a stop in front of the hotel. Sarah's legs were shaking, but she held her ground and walked toward the entranceway.

There were still people milling around from earlier, but she didn't linger. She just wanted to get back to her room and forget about what had happened between Luke and her.

"Sarah!"

She turned and Luke was headed toward her.

Just say good-night. Turn around and walk away.

Only she couldn't. She was so weak.

"Yeah?" she asked.

"Thank you for stitching up my head."

She nodded. "You should get that checked out later by Carson. Try not to get it wet. You probably know the drill when it comes to stitches."

He smiled. "I do, but thanks."

Turn around. Walk away.

"Will I see you tomorrow?"

You fool.

"Probably not. I have to get back up to Nestor's place and restock some stuff. I actually might rest for a couple of days."

"Of course. Take it easy and thanks for saving my life up there."

"I didn't save your life. You saved your own."

"If you hadn't shown me, I wouldn't have known what to do."

"If I hadn't shown you, you would've never been allowed to come up there with me," Luke said, and she realized his tone had changed. "You shouldn't have been up there with me."

"What are you talking about?" Sarah asked, confused. She'd thought he was happy that she'd gone up the mountain with him. He'd said so. What had changed? Why did he look so guilt-ridden?

Luke grabbed her by the arms, giving her a little shake. "You could've died in that avalanche."

"You could've, too."

He shook his head. "You could've died and it would've been my fault. I couldn't have borne that."

"I wanted to go with you."

Luke pushed her away and cursed under his breath. But she wasn't going to let him run away so she stood in front of him, blocking his path.

"I wanted to go with you," she stated again. "You said you were glad I was up there. You were glad to have the extra set of medically trained hands. You didn't force me up that mountain. It was my choice. Just like you couldn't have forced me down the mountain. You wanted me up there and I wanted to be there."

"What I wanted doesn't matter. It doesn't matter when it comes to your life. I won't be responsible for that."

And before she could say anything else to him he turned and walked away. She wanted to go after him, but she recognized that look.

He was going to retreat back up into the mountains. When he was ready, she'd see him again, but only when she was ready.

Right now, she wasn't ready to see him for a long time.

CHAPTER ELEVEN

SARAH HADN'T SEEN Luke in the week since they had spent the night together up in the cabin caught between a snowstorm and an avalanche. She'd been expecting it. Any time she got too close to Luke, he hid in the forest for a while.

It was the same with her.

Only she hid in her clinic.

She didn't regret what had happened between them. She'd wanted it. And she'd meant what she'd said about not promising anything to him. It had been only about the moment that night.

Only now she missed him and she wished they'd promised each other that it wouldn't be weird after. That they could still be friends. And she wished he didn't feel so guilty about putting her into a dangerous situation. It had been her choice. He had nothing to feel guilty about, but there had been no telling him that.

She'd gotten so used to him being around, his absence made her heart ache. Loneliness had never bothered her before, until now.

Though she didn't have much time to dwell on it. The hotel was busier than ever. As Valentine's Day and its grand opening approached more and more guests were coming to Crater Lake. Including a lot of wealthy A-listers. The population of Crater Lake went from just under six hundred people to more than a thousand overnight.

And it wasn't just Silas Draven's hotel that was selling out.

All the guest accommodations in town were full. Even privately owned rental cabins, which had never been rented during the winter season before, were full. Crater Lake was turning into a winter hotspot.

Sarah had been go, go, go since she came down off the mountain. Her clinic was busy with superficial stuff, stomach bugs and someone requesting a bikini wax and Botox, which she didn't do and promptly sent them to the on-site spa. She hadn't a moment to think for herself. So when she finally did get a break she headed to town to grab a cup of coffee and some peace and quiet.

As she walked down the street she spotted Esme in a stationery store and headed in to visit her. Esme was standing beside a large rack of Valentine's Day cards, mumbling to herself and frowning.

"You look like you're going to be sick," Sarah teased, coming up behind her.

"Oh, hey!" Esme laughed then. "I might. Did I mention that I hate Valentine's Day?"

"Yes. You mentioned something about that the first time we met. If you hate it so much, then why are you standing here in a shop that's overflowing with abomination?"

"Because my boyfriend likes Valentine's Day." She wrinkled her nose. "So I thought I would be nice and get him a card that I can shove in his face when he forces me to go to that Valentine's ball gala thing next week and makes me dress up like a princess or something very fluffy."

Sarah chuckled. "Not really romantic to shove something in someone's face and dressing up can be fun."

Esme grinned. "It depends on the dressing up, though."

"I don't know you well enough to talk about that." And they both laughed.

"He knows how much I hate it. He bought tickets just to annoy me." Esme pulled out a card. "This one is perfect. What do you think?"

The card in question had a large chimpanzee on it, making a kiss face. There was also faux fur glued to the outside. It was tacky and hideous, but Esme seemed so pleased with her find.

"That's an interesting choice. What does it say?"

"It says 'It's no monkey business, because I'm bananas for you.'" Esme grinned. "Yes, this is the one."

"That's a terrible card," Sarah said between chuckles. "It makes me cringe. Besides, that's clearly a chimpanzee and not a monkey, so really it's false advertising."

"Which is why it's so perfect. So, how are things with you?" Esme winked and Sarah groaned inwardly. What had she learned? Did Luke say anything and if so what did he say?

Just play it cool. Pretend as if nothing happened.

"I'm good."

"Good, huh? I hear your clinic has been busy."

"It has. More and more guests are arriving every day. A lot of big names."

Esme's expression hardened. "Hollywood A-listers?"

"Yeah, why?"

Esme sighed. "I used to run in that crowd before I

came here. It's not my favorite crowd. You know I was engaged to Dr. Draven's son."

"No. I didn't. Wait, you were engaged to Shane Draven? When?"

"A couple of years ago. I ended it and I fell out of grace with that group of people. I don't miss it at all."

Sarah nodded. She didn't miss the glitterati of Manhattan or the so-called friends she'd made in the circles of society her parents traveled in, because once you weren't in that circle anymore you became a ghost. Just a memory that was briefly touched upon during lulls in conversation.

"I couldn't agree more." Sarah picked up a card with a red heart. One thing she did miss about this time of year was when they would light up the Empire State Building with pink or red, sometimes even a heart.

"Have you seen the other Dr. Ralston lately?" Esme asked.

"Luke?"

"Yeah." There was a twinkle in her eye.

"Why?"

"No reason. I didn't mean to put you on the defensive. Carson told me what happened up there."

Sarah groaned. "Oh, he did?"

"Yeah. I can't even begin to imagine being caught in an avalanche. You were so lucky that you weren't swept away. Why, Glacier National Park had several avalanche-related deaths last year. It's scary. I never really thought about snow as a threat."

"You wouldn't—you come from California."

"I'm actually from Ohio originally. I have a respect for winter, but never seen an avalanche. Heck, until last summer I'd never really seen a landslide and apparently there's a dormant volcano around here."

Sarah laughed. "Guess we really did move to a danger zone."

Esme shrugged. "It's beautiful here, though. I love my life here. I wouldn't change it for anything."

Sarah nodded. "Well, I better head back to the hotel. I only had a small break and I'm sure there's another group of people wanting me to laser off their hair or inject them with silicone or something."

"I hope you're kidding?"

"I wish I was. Why they come to me instead of heading to the spa I can't understand."

She missed being a surgeon. She loved living in Crater Lake and the opportunity to work in Silas Draven's hotel was fantastic, but she missed the ER. For the first time in a long time, she actually missed the hustle and bustle of the ER.

She hadn't thought that she would when she'd first left active trauma surgery, when she'd taken on that job and started touring the country and training doctors. Despite what her father had done, she'd really enjoyed the travel and connections she'd made working with some of the finest surgeons in the world.

Returning back to the ER as a trauma surgeon had seemed like a step back, but now she realized that really this job was a step back. The only thing that really excited her was working with Luke. The bear mauling, the birth, even operating on Shane Draven last summer, all of those instances when she was called in to help in an emergency situation were when she felt like herself.

When she felt free.

And she missed it; she just hadn't realized how much

she had until now. She'd leave, but she had a contract to fulfill and she wouldn't back down. She finished things she started. On the other hand she didn't want to leave Crater Lake.

She didn't want to leave Luke.

"Well," Sarah said. "It was nice to see you again, but I have to head back."

Esme nodded and then reached out and squeezed her arm. "It was nice talking with you, too. Will I see you at the Valentine's ball?"

"Yes. I have to go. Silas Draven's orders. I would skip it since I have no one to go with and I'll probably be too busy the next day dealing with hangovers. It would be nice to get the extra sleep."

They both laughed at that. Sarah waved goodbye and headed back in the cold. If she could only remain in Crater Lake, but as an independent doctor, then she wouldn't mind that too much, but how many doctors did a small town need?

If she wanted to return to surgery, she'd have to leave Crater Lake.

It was as simple as that, but she might be persuaded to stay if Luke wanted her to. Even though that was very unlikely.

Luke was not ready for love and she doubted he would ever be.

She couldn't put her career on hold on the off chance Luke might want her. That was no way to live a life, so, as much as she hated the thought, once her year was up at Crater Lake she was going to find a hospital and go back to her first love of trauma surgery.

Even if it meant breaking her own heart in the process.

Then she thought of that painting he loved. The watercolor she'd done of the horse on the plains. She'd told him to take it, but he hadn't. Maybe she could give that to him as a peace offering.

If they couldn't be anything else, she wanted them to be friends. When she got back to the hotel she grabbed the painting and scrawled *For Adele* on the back before slipping it into an envelope.

Then she headed back to her clinic.

When she arrived she was surprised to find Luke pacing outside her office. The sight of him made her pulse quicken and she could recall every kiss of his lips on her skin, the weight of his body on her and the warmth. It had been over a week since she'd seen him, but looking at him now it felt as if it were just yesterday and that moment in the cabin came flooding back to her.

She both hated and loved the effect he had on her, but she was glad he was here. She'd missed him.

The only telltale sign that time had passed was that he'd had the stitches removed, but the gash had healed nicely, only leaving a small red mark barely visible at his hairline.

"Luke, what a surprise." And she held out the envelope ready to give it to him, but he didn't look at her.

"Where were you?" he snapped.

"In town. It was my morning off."

"I thought you would be here." He was clearly agitated.

"I'm here now. What're you so worked up about?"

Luke didn't say anything; he opened her clinic door, which she'd thought was locked, and dragged her inside, shutting the door behind them and locking it.

"What is up with you?" She tried to touch his laceration. "Do you want me to check your head?"

He grabbed her hand by the wrist and stopped her, shocking her, and then he let go of her hand, but didn't offer up an apology.

"It's not me," he said. "It's Nestor."

"Nestor?" She understood why he was so upset.

He's like a second father to me.

"Where is he? I'll see him right away."

Luke nodded and took her to one of the exam rooms, where Nestor was lying on a bed, pale and barely moving, cocooned in blankets. You could see the effects of chemotherapy. His face was gaunt, yellowish and there wasn't a hair on his face or head.

"What happened?" Sarah asked, setting the envelope down on the counter.

"I found him in a snowbank when I went up to cut some more wood for him. I don't know how long he's been out there. It's hypothermia—I think it's moderate. I knew I had to get him here. I would have administered warm IV fluids, but the cabinet is locked."

Sarah didn't question the fact he'd broken into her clinic and tried to break into her medicine cabinet. He was trying to save his friend's life. There was no time for arguments as she tossed Luke the key from her pocket.

"Not lactated Ringer's. With the chemo I don't know how well his liver is functioning and if he has hypothermia his liver might not be able to metabolize the lactate."

"I know," Luke called over his shoulder.

Sarah pulled out her stethoscope and the moment she touched him, he was cold, but, as she was taught in medical school, the patient was not dead until he was warm and dead. His temperature when she took it was twenty seven. Which was another reason she didn't want lactated Ringer's solution. He was too cold. He was heading toward profound hypothermia.

She tried to listen to the heart, but couldn't hear anything.

"Asystole!" Sarah shouted, then she felt the carotid artery; there was a faint thready pulse. "No, there's a pulse."

The heart was moving, but barely.

Luke came running back with bags of warmed IV fluid. "There's a pulse?"

"It's weak, so no CPR. Let's get the warm bolus into him."

Luke set up the IV and she grabbed warmers. Right now the most important thing was to heat his core; limbs could wait. The best way though to warm up a body that was this cold was cardiopulmonary bypass, but she was not equipped to do that here. Esme might be in town, but Nestor was here and they couldn't move him.

They could lose him if they took him out.

Hopefully the warmed IV would help, but given the state of Nestor's body, which had been ravaged by the chemotherapy, he didn't have much of a shot.

"Come on, Nestor," Luke whispered to the old man. "Come on. You're not going to go out like this. You said you wanted to go out riding a bear like a horse off the side of a cliff. This is not the way to go."

Sarah's heart broke as she watched Luke gingerly touch the old man's face. She knew Nestor was important to Luke, because Nestor had taught him how to survive in the mountains. It pained Sarah to see Luke like this, but there was not a lot she could do here with severe hypothermia.

Watching Luke beg his friend to keep fighting brought

tears to her eyes. Here, in this moment, Luke was so raw, so real.

This was the genuine Luke Ralston. Not the lone wolf everyone else saw. This tender, concerned Luke, begging the man he admired so much to hang on, was the man she longed to know.

The man who could feel.

The man who could teach her how to feel.

As she watched the two of them she knew that she didn't have that kind of parent-child relationship with her parents and probably never would.

It made her sad to watch Luke suffer so much. She didn't have the heart to tell him that Nestor might not make it. Though she probably didn't have to tell him that. He probably already knew.

"Did you call the air ambulance?" Sarah asked.

"I did, but we have to warm him up before we can get him out to meet the ambulance."

She nodded, but didn't say anything.

When a patient's core temperatures were below thirty, they required to be rewarmed internally through cardiopulmonary bypass, gastric lavage and other means. Ways that Sarah couldn't provide for him in this private clinic.

Usually people that severe were taken straight to the hospital where aggressive rewarming could start instantly. All they could do with what she had was blankets, heaters and the IV. She took Nestor's temperature again, but it was dropping fast.

She knew what was going to happen next. His heart would stop completely and if they rewarmed him too fast, his heart could collapse, but she couldn't use CPR to keep the brain alive until after he was asystole.

"What's his temperature?"

Sarah sighed. "Twenty-five. Luke, the lowest someone has come back from such a severe hypothermia is thirteen point seven."

"He'll make it."

She listened for cardiac activity, but there was none that she could make out. She felt for the carotid artery and the pulse was gone. He wasn't warm enough to start CPR, but she had no choice.

"Starting CPR. Get the AED."

Luke nodded as she began CPR.

Come on, Nestor. Don't die here. Don't die on me.

Luke got the AED ready and Sarah stopped CPR while Luke shocked Nestor. There was no response. Sarah continued with the CPR and they alternated.

"Nestor, come on," Luke urged.

When she looked at the clock, she could see that they'd been doing CPR for far too long. The ambulance had still not arrived.

"Take his temperature," Sarah said as she continued CPR.

"Dammit, it's fourteen."

Come on, Nestor.

"I can't pronounce him but..."

"Don't say it," Luke begged. "Don't. People survive hypothermia all the time. Cancer kills, but hypothermia can be cured."

Sarah sighed, and continued, but there wasn't much hope. Luke turned his back on the scene. His fists clenched as she worked on. He obviously couldn't stand to watch his friend slip away.

She didn't have any hope...and then Nestor's heart came back under her hand and he groaned, before coughing.

"Oh, my God," she whispered.

Nestor opened one eye, groaned, and passed out again. But the point was, he was alive.

"What?" Luke asked, then leaned over. His eyes widened in shock. "You got him back?"

Sarah had never brought back a person with such severe hypothermia, with a body already so weakened by chemo, from the brink of death. Tears of joy stung her eyes and she laughed out loud because she couldn't contain herself.

Luke smiled at her briefly before turning back to his friend.

She was so relieved. She hadn't wanted to be the one responsible for not saving Nestor's life. She hadn't wanted to hurt Luke like that, and she hadn't wanted him to be reminded of Nestor's death every time he saw her.

She didn't want Luke to remember her like that.

"You brought him back," Luke said, stunned. "I've never seen that."

"I've never done it in this situation before. And especially not outside a hospital."

"I can't believe you did it."

Nestor was still unconscious, but he was stable, and when she took a temperature again it was rising. He had a good shot at making it now.

The paramedics came then and took over, Sarah gave an update about Nestor's temperature and how long he'd been down. They were going to take Nestor to the hospital and continue to warm him up, but Nestor wasn't out of the woods yet. Chemo took its toll. As did Nestor's age.

She followed the paramedics down out of her clinic and made sure Nestor was in the air ambulance and on his way.

Luke stood beside her, his expression unreadable and his gaze trained on the ambulance as it disappeared from view and on to the nearest hospital. There they could work on him. They walked back up to the clinic to clean up the mess.

Luke cursed under his breath as he picked up Nestor's hat, which had fallen on the floor of the exam room. His eyes were wild, but he wasn't about to cry. It was rage she saw there.

That brief moment of tenderness and joy after she'd saved Nestor's life had faded away. Luke's walls had gone back up again. Like armor.

She wanted to tell him that he didn't need to guard himself in front of her.

He could be himself.

How can he be himself when you can't be yourself?

Sarah touched Luke's arm. "I'm so sorry that happened to him. I wonder what caused him to collapse in the snow."

He shrugged it off. "People don't die from hypothermia and he won't either."

"They do, Luke. You don't know how long he was in the snow for. Or how he even got there. He's alive, but with chemo…his body's been through a trauma."

He scrubbed a hand over his face. "What I meant was that people don't die of hypothermia on my watch. They don't. No man gets left behind. Every life gets saved. Nestor has fought cancer, he can fight this."

"Is that what you would tell yourself in the army?"

His gaze was positively flinty. "What?"

"Why did you leave the army, Luke? It's clear to me you're so passionate about it, why would you leave it?"

Luke snorted and tried to push past her. "I don't have time for this."

"Of course you don't. You never do."

"What's that supposed to mean?"

Sarah shook her head. "It means you'll disappear off into the forest, like you always do, and when you're done sulking you'll come back and pretend like nothing happened. I can't deal with that kind of hot and cold, Luke. I won't deal with that."

"How do you expect me to act, Sarah? A friend of mine almost died. Never leave a man behind, that's the way I've always lived and yet..." He trailed off and then shook his head. "I'm done. I can't deal with this. This is why I keep to myself. This is pointless."

He turned and started to walk away.

"It is. You're a coward, Luke."

He spun around. "I'm the coward? How do you figure that?"

"You're a coward because you won't let anyone in. You won't let anyone help you. I'm sorry you were burned before by people you care about. I'm sorry that you've lost people important to you, but you can't run away from your fears. You have to face them."

"Is that a fact?" He crossed his arms. "And what do you think you're doing here?"

Honestly, she didn't know. She didn't know why she was bothering with him. He clearly didn't want her involved in his life. She should know better.

She was better off alone. Then she only had to answer to herself for her own actions and mistakes. Maybe Luke had it right.

"Working and trying to save lives."

"I mean why are you in Crater Lake? You gave up a

prominent job because you were afraid you weren't good enough. You were afraid that everyone would think you were just riding on Daddy's coattails. You ran away from your talent. You're just as much a coward as I am."

"You're a jerk." She threw the envelope at him. "This was for you, because I thought we were friends. Clearly, I was wrong."

Luke touched his face where the envelope had hit him, snickered and then walked away from her. His words had stung, as if he'd cut her open with a scalpel, but then the truth did hurt. It hurt all the more that it came from him.

Someone she'd thought she could trust enough to tell her darkest fear to. She'd never told anyone else that she'd given up the job because her father had gotten it for her. That was her shame to bear. She'd thought Luke would understand, but she was wrong.

Then again, she was wrong about a lot of other things. This was no different.

CHAPTER TWELVE

"LUKE, I KNOW you're in there. I can see you."

Luke looked over at the window to see his brother peering through. He'd thought that if he retreated to Nestor's cabin, to clean up a bit and close it up until Nestor could come and claim it, it would help get his mind off the fact that he'd probably broken the heart of the woman he loved.

When he'd said those things to Sarah, the moment they'd slipped from his lips he'd realized what a mistake he'd made. That this time, he'd hurt someone he cared about, but she would move on. Like Christine had and he would be the only one with a broken heart.

It served him right.

Sarah hadn't made any promises the night they made love. That was what he'd thought he wanted; that was what he always wanted. He didn't want any commitments. He didn't want anyone to love, but the problem was she'd gotten underneath his skin.

When she was working so hard to save Nestor's life, when she thought it was completely hopeless, she still fought and she was doing it for him. And she'd brought him back. He knew that. Sarah did the best she could with what she had. She could've turned him away, but she hadn't. She wasn't that kind of person and he admired her for it, but Sarah was not meant to be his.

She deserved so much more. He'd hurt her, dragged her into dangerous situations and he demanded so much of her.

Sarah was better off without him.

He didn't deserve love.

Luke didn't know anything about love. He hadn't been able to keep Christine happy when they were married. He'd chosen his career over her. She hadn't wanted to live in Germany. She hadn't wanted to live in a cabin in the woods, yet he'd been selfish and tried to have it his way.

No wonder Christine had left him.

How could he have love, deserve love, if he couldn't change or bend, too? It was too hard, too painful. The problem was, Sarah had somehow snuck in and captured his heart. He didn't know how, but she had.

Of course, that was all ruined now.

He'd taken that piece of her, the one she'd shared with him, and thrown it back in her face. He'd used it to hurt her. To drive her away. So, no, he didn't deserve love. She'd given him that horse painting, as well. Another piece of her she'd shared with him that he'd tossed back at her like garbage.

He hated himself for it.

He'd made his bed and he was going to lie in it.

Of course, coming back to Nestor's cabin was a huge mistake. Not only because it made him emotional, thinking about the friend he'd almost lost, but also because it reminded him of being in her arms. When she kissed him, when she opened herself up to him. The night they became one. That night he was lost to her because she entrusted him with a piece of her.

Now he'd shattered her heart.

Her words might have stung him, but he'd deserved it because the unseen wound he'd inflicted on her was a thousand times worse.

He'd seen her once in town. He'd wanted to tell her that Nestor had pulled through, that they had managed to warm him with lavage, but she hadn't looked at him. She hadn't said anything to him. She had been silent, which was odd for her. Since they first met she'd always been frank about what she thought about him.

The cold shoulder had been too much for him to bear. Even though he'd deserved it. So he'd retreated back to the mountains, under the guise that he was cleaning up Nestor's cabin for the family, but really he just wanted to be alone and mend the broken heart he'd caused himself because he let Sarah in and then pushed her away.

You don't know if she loved you back.

Which was true, but it didn't make the pain better and was pointless now, because he'd completely ruined it. Then he glanced at the painting on the mantel where he'd placed it when he came up here. The horse that looked like Adele. Something she'd painted herself; he could see her slender, graceful hand in each delicate brush stroke. Detailed and precise, as a brilliant surgeon should be. It was a piece of her and just knowing that hurt all the more.

"Luke, it's cold out here. Let me in." Carson's shouting from outside interrupted his train of thought.

Luke groaned and got up to open the door. Carson burst past him and stomped his feet at the door.

"What're you doing here, Carson?"

"Looking for you. After Nestor's accident, you disappeared."

Luke shrugged. "I came up here to clean it up. Nestor's

son Greg won't be back up here until spring, possibly summer. I wanted to make sure nothing would go bad. I wanted to make sure everything was squared away. Nestor's lucky to be alive. He'll be in the hospital for a while."

Carson nodded. "Right."

"What's that supposed to mean?"

"Exactly what you think it means."

Luke cursed. "I don't have time for this."

"Why? Because you're so busy up here moping?"

Luke glared at Carson, but his little brother was holding his ground and looking quite smug about it.

"What are you grinning about?"

"I'm thinking back to a conversation we had this summer. Do you remember that particular conversation?"

"No."

Which was a lie. Luke vaguely remembered it. He remembered his brother coming to get him in Missoula, struggling with the fact that he was in love with Esme and was scared of getting a broken heart. Scared of possibly walking away from a family practice, because Carson had put it on himself to carry on the family legacy in Crater Lake.

Luke had told him, in a nutshell, to snap out of it and live.

And now the jerk was throwing it back in his face.

Typical.

"I believe you said to me, and I quote, 'Forgive yourself. And for once follow your heart. Do what you want to do. Live.' Wasn't that the line you fed me?"

"It sounds vaguely familiar."

"You're an idiot. You also told me, 'She'll walk away,

she's going to walk away and you know who I'm talking about,' and now it applies to you."

"Do you have an eidetic memory or something?"

"No. I just stored those particular lines away for future blackmail and use."

Luke rolled his eyes. "I said those words to you because you deserved Esme. She loved you and you love her."

"Sarah loves you and you're an idiot if you think any different."

Luke shook his head. "You don't know what you're talking about."

"And I'll say it again, you're an idiot."

"I don't deserve love. I blew my first marriage because I was too selfish. And this time around I shut her out because I didn't want to get hurt. It was selfish. I threw it away. For me, love is pointless."

Carson sighed. "Luke, you gave up the army for her. That doesn't sound like someone who is selfish."

"I should've given it up earlier."

"Why? Christine knew your passion for the army before you were married to her. She was just as selfish as you. You gave up the army for her, you tried for her. She ruined it. She found happiness, why can't you? You deserve happiness."

"No. I don't. Maybe it was all me. I can't take the risk again. I don't want to take the risk again. It's better that she leaves. It's better she walks."

Carson took him by the shoulders and shook him. "I love you, but you're an idiot."

"So you've said."

"I'll say it again, like you said it to me. Forgive yourself. Take a chance and live. You love her. You may not admit it, but I can see it as plain as day."

Luke walked away from his brother and sat down on the edge of Nestor's bunk, running his hands through his hair. His hand brushing over the tender scar from the laceration Sarah had stitched up.

That was one of the scariest moments of his life, when he saw that avalanche raging down the side of the mountain toward them and saw the look of horror on her face. All he could do was tell her to do what he'd taught her. In that moment he didn't care much about his life. Only hers, because he couldn't bear it if he lost her.

Yet, he had lost her.

He'd driven her away.

Carson was right. He was an idiot.

"You've realized what a moron you are now." Carson was grinning ear to ear.

"I thought I was an idiot?"

Carson shrugged. "Both, I think."

Luke laughed. "Yeah, you're right."

"I know what happened between you and Christine was bad and the fact that she ran off with Anthony sucks. It does, but you said so yourself, you wanted different things. I think you and Sarah want the same things."

"And what would that be?"

"She's a trauma surgeon and so are you. You're a great first responder, Luke, but you have to get off the mountain and become a surgeon again. Don't you remember what it was like in the OR? I know you loved it. I remember the emails. You were born to be a surgeon. You are a surgeon, you just stopped practicing."

"I don't think she wants to be a surgeon anymore. She left that life behind her."

"She thinks she has. She's a surgeon. Just go live. Do you think that soldier who died would want you mourning his death for the rest of your life? No. Go live your life, Luke."

The words sank in slowly.

He'd been blaming himself so long for his heartache that he didn't realize he'd given up the thing he'd loved the most and that was surgery. He was so busy trying to rescue everyone that he didn't see that he was the one who needed rescuing. He was going to make it up to Sarah. He was going to win her back, even if he didn't know how exactly or if he ever would, but he was going to try.

He couldn't live without her. Of that he was certain.

Luke got up and clapped Carson on the back. "Thanks."

"No problem. I just hope she forgives you." Carson winked. "Now, are you coming down off this mountain? Tomorrow is Valentine's Day. I think that's a perfect time to make up."

"I don't have tickets to that dance," Luke said.

Carson reached in his pocket. "You can have mine. Esme and I aren't going to that dance. I suspect tomorrow we'll have more important things to celebrate."

Luke cocked an eyebrow. "Like what?"

"I'm proposing to Esme tonight. She has no idea."

He grinned. "It's Friday the thirteenth. You know that, right?"

Carson chuckled. "I know, but she really hates Valentine's Day. I mean really hates it. I found a card with a chimp on it."

Luke shook his head. "Would you get out of here? I'll come down off the mountain in time for tomorrow."

"Good." Carson punched him on the shoulder. "Good luck."

"You, too. It's about time you did that, by the way."

"What?"

"Propose to Esme."

Carson snorted. "Look who's talking."

Sarah's heart hurt. It had been a few days since she'd last seen Luke in town briefly. It had looked as if he'd wanted to talk to her, but he'd turned away. He'd looked pale and emotionless. Several times she'd talked herself out of going over to him and comforting him, because really what good would it do?

He would just push her away.

You need to fight harder.

She let out another sigh, because she was all out of fight. How could she fight for the man she was in love with when she couldn't even stand up to her parents? Luke had been right, she should've stayed in that job she'd thought she earned and proven to them she was more than a name.

Even though she'd saved Nestor's life, she'd done so much good here and she wanted more.

She missed the OR.

She missed the chaos of a busy emergency room, the beauty of an OR being prepped by scrub nurses, the feel of the water on her arms as she scrubbed in and the calm she felt as she waited for the patient to go under and the magic of saving a life.

Being around Luke reminded her of that.

How long had she just been walking through the paces of life and not living it?

A long time.

With Luke, she mattered and working with him made her realize she was a damn good surgeon in her own right. As soon as her yearlong contract was up, she was going to find an ER job again. Even if it meant she wasn't running the ER, she still wanted to be where she belonged. She'd known the moment she'd picked up her first scalpel that she didn't belong in her parents' penthouse on the Upper West Side.

Just as she didn't belong in a clinic treating minor injuries.

She belonged down on the front lines and on the surgical floor.

Just as she and Luke belonged together, even if he didn't think they did. She'd never fallen in love before, but, with him, she fell hard and the answer was simple. He brought out the best in her. He made her work harder than she'd ever worked before.

Around him, she felt like herself and she hadn't felt like herself in a very long time. She was so busy distancing herself from her parents, trying to step out of their shadows to prove that she didn't need them, that she didn't realize she'd blocked out everyone.

Including herself.

"Excuse me, are you still open? I know it's four o'clock on Friday and your clinic states you're only open until four, but I'm hoping you can see me."

Sarah looked up from her chart and saw a middle-aged woman, guarding her side, standing in the doorway. She seemed vaguely familiar, but perhaps she'd treated her earlier.

"Of course. Come in."

The woman looked relieved and followed Sarah into an exam room.

"Why don't you have a seat, Ms…?"

"It's Mrs. Vargas, but I can't sit, I'm afraid. I fell while I was skiing and I'm terrified I broke a rib."

Sarah smiled. "It must've been a nasty fall."

"It was. I've never skied before, but my husband insisted we come here for a romantic Valentine's weekend, when really I should be back in Great Falls and working."

"What do you do, Mrs. Vargas?"

"I'm the head of a board of directors for a hospital. We've scouted an area just outside of Crater Lake to build a small hospital that deals mostly with trauma. There's a serious lag around here. Missoula and Great Falls sees most of the trauma, but those locations are too far away to do any help."

"So you're going to build a hospital that only deals with trauma?"

She nodded and then winced. "I'm sorry for boring you, but I thought you might be interested in that seeing how you're a doctor and everything."

"You're not boring me. I totally agree this area is seriously lacking in a trauma center. I can only do so much here."

"Well, I know there's a cardiac surgeon in town and we've offered her use of our operating rooms. It's just a matter of finding a trauma surgeon for next year."

"Well, Mrs. Vargas, you don't have a broken rib."

"Are you sure?"

Sarah nodded. "Positive. If you had a fracture in your ribs you wouldn't be talking to me so easily. You're guarding, but I suspect you've given yourself a nasty bruise. Inhale deeply for me."

Mrs. Vargas did that.

"Did it hurt or was it hard to do?"

"No."

"I'll prescribe you some painkillers, but rest now and put some ice on it."

Mrs. Vargas nodded as she filled out the prescription

and handed it to her. Mrs. Vargas stared at it. "Ledet? Are you related to Vin Ledet from New York?"

Sarah groaned inwardly. "Yes. He's my father. Do you know him?"

"No, I just remember someone telling me that Vin Ledet's daughter was a brilliant trauma surgeon. They said you saved their life last summer. Who was it? Oh, yes, Shane Draven. His uncle owns this hotel."

"I really can't say brilliant, but I was that trauma surgeon. I did work on Shane, but he came to me in stable condition thanks to both Dr. Ralstons and Dr. Petersen, who tended to him in the field. I just happened to be a locum surgeon in Missoula, throwing in a hand during a busy stint."

"Well, you're not blowing your own horn. Shane Draven spoke very highly of your skills." Mrs. Vargas pulled out a business card. "If you're interested in returning to an ER and running it as chief of surgery, please do call me."

Chief?

"I think you'd want someone more experienced?"

"The way Shane talks about you I'd say you're experienced enough. I did do a quick background check on you, before realizing you were here. Everyone speaks highly of you as a surgeon."

Sarah blushed. "Thank you, Mrs. Vargas."

"Will I see you tomorrow at the Valentine's Day dance? I would like to introduce you to some members of the board."

"*I* will be at the dance. Silas Draven wants all his staff there, but I don't want to see *you* at that dance. Are we clear?"

Mrs. Vargas winked. "Very well. Please do think

about my offer. I would love to have a surgeon of your caliber in charge of this project."

Sarah walked Mrs. Vargas out and when she'd left, Sarah stared at the card for a long time. The offer came because of Shane Draven, not her father. Mrs. Vargas was aware of who her father was, but it was her own merit that preceded her. Not her father pulling strings.

She would take the job to stay in Crater Lake. She loved it here.

She was making friends here.

She was finding her place in this world, when for so long she'd felt as if she was drifting.

Here she wasn't Vin Ledet's daughter. Here she was a surgeon, a doctor. She'd found herself and she'd been foolish not to look sooner. She'd been so busy trying to show her parents who she wasn't that she couldn't show them who she was.

She didn't have to prove anything to them, because there was nothing to prove. Their opinion of her was never going to change and, for the first time in a long time, she was okay with that.

Chief of surgery sounded like a dream job. And she could stay in Crater Lake.

What's keeping you in Crater Lake?

And that realization made her sad.

Luke had made it clear how he felt about love. He thought it was pointless and he'd shut her out. She didn't want to remain in a town where he was.

She loved him too much and it was clear that he didn't return those feelings. So the best thing to do after her contract was up was make a clean break, for both of them.

Even though a clean break was the last thing she

wanted, because all she wanted was to be his. To be by his side and in his arms.

She was in love with him and she doubted that feeling would disappear anytime soon, but Luke loved Crater Lake. This was his home. It wasn't her home, even if she wanted it to be. So she'd leave.

Because she loved him so much, she'd leave and let him get on with his life without her. She could find roots in another town, even though she loved Crater Lake.

And she would find another job and of that she had no doubt now.

CHAPTER THIRTEEN

A MONTH AGO you couldn't have paid him enough to be at a gala like this. All the people, the drinking, the noise and decorations were enough to set him on edge. Luke didn't really like being around people who pretended to be nice. Who were putting on a show.

He avoided social situations like this for a reason.

So, no, he wouldn't be at an event like this, not for all the money in the world, but for Sarah he'd walk through fire. For her he'd do anything. She deserved it all and if she let him, if she forgave him, he would spend every waking moment making it up to her.

Since Christine left him he'd always stated his only mistress was the mountain, but the mountain was cold. So cold his heart had been frozen.

Until Sarah came.

Now all he wanted was her and he was going to do everything and anything to get her back.

She was across the room now and he caught glimpses of her through all the people. She was so close, but so far away. To get to her, it would be like walking through fire for him.

He waited until she was alone and not talking with

Silas Draven. He didn't want anyone to interrupt this moment.

Carson and Esme had helped him get ready, since the only suit he owned was from when he was eighteen and married to Christine. So that was unacceptable, coupled with the fact it no longer fit him.

So he wore Carson's suit. It was designer and, even though he felt completely awkward in it, Esme had swooned over him. He knew then it was good. That he would fit in for her. He'd even shaved his beard off.

Now he stood on the other side of the gala, remaining in the shadows at the edge of the dance floor watching her. She took his breath away. She was wearing a bloodred, sparkling evening gown that was a halter, so he got to admire her creamy white shoulders, but the seller for him was her white-blond hair was pulled to one side, but down. So it just brushed the top of her shoulder. Just like in that self-portrait she'd done. The one he loved the most.

Of course, when he was presented with the real thing, the drawing paled in comparison. Sarah was beautiful. She was radiant and he noticed other men admiring her, which ticked him off, but no one else approached her. So he didn't have to inflict any bodily harm on would-be suitors.

She looked unhappy standing off to the side and he knew that was his fault. Something he aimed to fix in a moment, because right now he just enjoyed the sight of her. He enjoyed drinking it in. He didn't want to disrupt the magic she was weaving.

He didn't deserve her, but he would work hard to rectify that for the rest of his life. If she would only let him, and he hoped she would. He pulled at his tie and headed toward her.

Luke had faced many dangerous situations in his life. Things that would scare others, but here, in this moment, crossing a dance floor to beg forgiveness and put his fragile heart on the line for the woman he loved was the scariest thing he'd ever done. But for her, he would do anything.

Sarah didn't want to be at this dance. Mostly because everyone who was at this gala was with someone and she was standing off to the side of the dance floor in her red evening gown, like a wallflower. It was like junior high all over again.

Still, it was a great success. She could see this Valentine's Gala becoming a yearly event for the hotel.

Valentine's never really bothered her, but right now watching all the happy couples dance, kiss and enjoy themselves made her envious.

She should just leave.

Silas Draven had introduced her to all his important guests and then she'd discreetly snuck away, wandering along the edge of the dance floor as the band played endless romantic songs. She was hoping that Esme would be here tonight, so at least maybe she could talk to someone she knew, but Esme hadn't shown up and Sarah hoped that it wasn't because of that goofy chimpanzee card she'd picked out.

The thought of that card made her laugh to herself. A waiter walked by with a tray full of champagne flutes. Sarah took one and as she glanced back across the dance floor her breath caught in her throat at the sight of a man in a well-tailored tuxedo walking across the floor toward her.

And it wasn't just any man. It was Luke and he was clean shaven.

Oh, my God.

Her knees buckled. Those intense blue eyes fixed on her as if he were going to devour her whole and devour her in a good way. A way that made her blood heat with need, with a craving she'd been trying to suppress since he'd walked away from her and broken her heart.

His beard was gone and she could clearly see those delectable lips, which had kissed every inch of her, turning up in a mischievous smile. He stopped in front of her and pulled on the cuff of his jacket, adjusting what looked like cuff links. His brown curls were tamed in a debonair coif, he had a tie on and it didn't look like a clip-on. He rolled his neck and pulled at the tie again. He must be so uncomfortable.

Good.

Even his boots were gone, replaced by dress shoes.

He spun around. "How do I look?"

So good. Only she didn't say that thought out loud. "Fine."

He cocked any eyebrow. "Just fine?"

No, she wasn't going to be drawn in by his cute banter. She wasn't going to let herself be drawn in by him again. She couldn't.

"I… What're you doing here?"

"I've come to the gala. Am I not dressed appropriately?"

"You're dressed fine. I told you that."

It's more than fine.

In fact she was having a hard time controlling herself

from throwing the champagne flute aside, hiking up her long skirt and jumping in his arms, but she controlled herself. She was angry at him.

"Can I have this dance?" He held out his hand, his blue eyes twinkling.

Say no. Say no.

"Okay." She took his hand and he led her out on the dance floor, spinning her around gracefully before pulling her back up against him. "I didn't know you could dance."

"I have hidden depths."

"I'm aware of those hidden depths," she said sarcastically. "I don't know why I'm dancing with you."

"Because you're a forgiving sort of person."

"Am I?"

"I think so."

"I hope you're right. I don't feel so forgiving right now."

"I loved my painting. I put it on the wall," he said changing the subject.

Her heart skipped a beat. "You did?"

Don't fall for it.

Only she couldn't help it when it came to Luke Ralston. She was so weak when it came to him.

He nodded. "Thank you for that. It's beautiful, but that wasn't my favorite the night you showed me your drawings."

"It wasn't?"

"No, it was the self-portrait you'd done." Then he reached out and ran his hands gently through her hair and brushed her shoulder. "It was the pencil drawing with your hair down, your shoulders bare. That's the drawing I loved."

Her pulse thundered in her ears. That was a drawing she'd always hated. One she'd never got right. At least she didn't think so. Maybe because she couldn't truly see herself through her own eyes. She was her own worst judge. But looking into Luke's eyes at this moment, in his arms, she could see what he saw, even if only for a brief moment, and it almost made her cry.

"Why didn't you tell me?"

"I didn't want you to know at the time."

She blushed. "I'm surprised you're here. I thought you didn't like Valentine's Day. It's the one thing you and Esme have in common."

"Me, too, to be honest." He chuckled. "Actually, Esme may be warming up to Valentine's Day, or at least Friday the thirteenth."

"Why?"

"Carson proposed last night and Esme accepted."

Sarah smiled. "Oh, how wonderful. I'm happy for her. I'm surprised they're not here celebrating."

"Well, they wanted me to come here."

She blushed again, her heart racing. "So what're you doing here?"

"I've come to beg for forgiveness."

Her heart skipped a beat. "What?"

"I've been an idiot. I thought love was pointless, but only for me."

"Only for you?"

He nodded. "My first wife left me because I was selfish. I was so focused on what I wanted that I didn't let her have a say. I wanted to be in the army and serve my country as a surgeon, I wanted to train at the army hospital in Germany and nothing was going to stop me. Not even the woman I loved, or thought I loved at the time. Actually, I'm surprised she didn't leave me sooner."

"I understand that kind of drive. You loved serving your country, so why did you leave it?"

"Because I left for her, but by then it was too late. I gave up my commission, but it wasn't enough. So I turned to the mountain. Being alone meant I could live my life the way I wanted. I never wanted to feel that pain or be responsible for inflicting that kind of pain on someone. I thought it was easier to shut people out. To be alone, and then you came along."

Tears stung her eyes. "Oh, Luke. Things aren't so black-and-white."

"I know that now. When you walked into that OR last summer, I knew there was something about you. I knew that you would break through, even if I didn't want to admit it. I love you, Sarah. I'll go wherever you need me to go. If you need to be a surgeon in New York again, I'll go there. I just can't lose you. I need you. I'll change my life, give up everything to be with you."

Her knees went weak and she wasn't sure she'd heard him correctly. No one had ever offered to give up everything to make her happy.

Everyone expected pieces of her, for her to conform, but Luke was offering all of himself to her and she was overwhelmed by it.

She knew there were tears running down her face but there was no stopping them.

"For so long I've been fighting to prove to the world I'm not someone they think I am, I didn't know who I really was, but with you I found who I was again. I shut everyone out. Even me. I shut myself out. I was convinced I didn't need love. That I didn't want love…that I could make it through this life on my own. I was wrong. I love you, Luke. I love you so much it hurts. You see me."

He pulled her tight against him, cupping her face, and then kissed her. His kiss gentle at first, before it deepened. She melted into that kiss, wrapping her arms around his neck, not caring who saw her kissing him. Her whole world had righted itself. She was where she wanted to be. She was who she wanted to be.

She had found out who she was thanks to this man.

When the kiss ended she laid her head against his shoulder, moving with him as they swayed gently on the dance floor. She didn't want to let him go. She'd missed him. She'd missed this Luke Ralston. A man she'd only met in brief glimpses. A man who had been surrounded by high walls.

A man she desperately wanted to love.

"So am I forgiven?" he teased.

"Yes. Though I should've made you work harder."

"Yes. You should've."

"Now you tell me." She glanced up at him and kissed him again. "Thank you for coming here tonight. This is the best apology ever."

"So, where should we move to?" Luke asked. "There's no surgical jobs in Crater Lake sadly."

"There will be next year when my contract is up here at the hotel."

"What?" He was clearly confused. "There's no hospital in Crater Lake. They talked once last year about building one, but nothing ever came of it."

"Not yet. A trauma and surgical center is going up outside of town. A board of directors from a large hospital in Great Falls realized there was a shortfall up in this area for one."

Luke grinned. "You want to stay in Crater Lake?"

"Of course. It's home now. You're my home." And it was true. She'd found a home. She'd found what she was looking for. She'd found herself in him.

Luke kissed her again. "And you're mine. I love you, Sarah."

Sarah kissed him back. "Happy Valentine's Day, Dr. Ralston."

EPILOGUE

Valentine's Day, a year later

SARAH WALKED SWIFTLY through the halls of the new trauma center. Her ER was running smoothly. Her board was in good working order, which made her slightly apprehensive. She'd learned early on as a trauma resident that a smoothly run ER and good board would mean that a huge trauma was due any second to muck it all up.

They'd only been open a month, but already there had been several large traumas, a couple of emergency births and an avalanche. Thankfully no bear mauling.

Sarah shuddered recalling that moment.

The man had pulled through, but required several plastic surgeries.

She'd seen several bears in the summer when Luke was working on building onto his cabin. Their cabin. And a bear had crashed Esme and Carson's wedding that summer, but thankfully none of the encounters had been violent.

Once she'd got the trauma center open, her father had come to tour the facility and he'd donated money to the pro bono fund, which had shocked her, but what was the most shocking moment was when he told her he was proud of her. That she had done well for herself.

And she had.

She was happier than she could ever remember.

Now, if only her boards would stay quiet tonight.

"Dr. Ledet, can you come to OR Four? There's a problem."

Sarah saw a very pregnant Esme running toward her. Esme operated on her cardio patients at the trauma center, but Sarah wondered when she was going to give it up because soon she'd be giving birth.

"You shouldn't be running," Sarah said. "You're due in, like, three weeks. Why are you even working now?"

"It's only an angio," Esme said, as if an angio were nothing. Which was odd for her.

Sarah glanced up at the board and then back to her. "You said there was a problem. If it's only a simple angio, then what's the problem?"

Esme bit her lip. "Oh, I'm not in OR Four. I'm in Three. That board is wrong. I finished my angio, but I was passing OR Four and they were having a problem."

Speak of a quiet board, get swift retribution.

"Okay, let's go." Sarah jogged behind Esme. They put on their surgical caps and then scrubbed. "So what's wrong again?"

"It was a mauling," Esme said. "It's pretty bad."

"Oh, no. Are you serious? Why do tourists insist on disturbing a bear during its hibernation cycle?" She walked into the OR, her hands up and waiting to get gloved when she saw Luke, gowned and standing in the OR alone.

"Bears don't hibernate, Sarah. Have I not taught you anything?"

Sarah glanced back, but Esme had disappeared. "What's going on here? I thought there was a mauling."

"No, no mauling, but I wanted to get you here fast, without arousing your suspicions."

"Well, now I'm suspicious. You're supposed to be in Missoula visiting Nestor. What's going on?"

"Nothing is going on."

"Is Nestor okay?" Sarah asked.

"He's fine. I swear. He hates city living, but you know that."

Sarah sighed in relief. She was glad to hear the older man was okay. She'd grown fond of him and went with Luke to visit him every month.

"So what's going on?" She asked.

"Well, picture this room full of rose petals." Luke grinned. "Only I know it's not."

"Which is good because if it was I would have a panic attack thinking about having to sterilize this OR again top to bottom. Do you know how many patients are allergic to scents?"

Luke crossed his arms. "Really? Don't you have any scope of imagination?"

"No, not on a night when the ER is quiet and my board *was* running smoothly."

Luke moved to stand in front of her. "Well, I was trying to be romantic, but I realize now it's kind of hard to be romantic when we're both wearing surgical masks standing in an OR."

"Yeah, why are we here?"

"Because it was in OR like this that I first met you. You told me to get out of your OR."

"And I'm telling you that now, too." She laughed nervously and then it hit her when she spied Esme in the scrub room, crying. "Oh, my God."

Luke got down on one knee and pulled out a ring. "Don't worry, it's been sterilized. It won't contaminate this surgical field."

"Oh, my God," she said again in disbelief.

"Sarah, I can't live without you. You brought me back from the dead. You taught me to love again, to feel again and I want you to be my wife. Marry me."

She began to cry, soaking the paper surgical mask. "Yes. I'll marry you. Yes!"

Luke slipped the ring on her finger. "Good. Nestor will be thrilled I finally found the nerve to ask you."

Sarah laughed. "Remind me to kiss him next time I see him."

"Kiss him?" Luke asked then ripped off his mask. "Sorry, but you're going to have to sterilize this OR again. I need to kiss my fiancée properly."

Sarah removed her mask and let him kiss her. It wasn't the exact OR where they'd first met, but it was an OR where they worked together constantly, together saving lives, but most of all it was a place where they'd saved each other.

And being in his arms was right where she needed to be.

"There's something else I need to tell you," Sarah said. "It's important."

Luke groaned, but grinned. "You want to move back to New York."

"No. Look, it's..."

A tap on the glass interrupted their conversation and she turned around to see Esme in the scrub room looking quite distressed.

"What's up with her?" Luke asked.

Esme hit the intercom. "Um, I think we need to sterilize that room right now. My water just broke."

Sarah chuckled as Esme was pointing frantically at her belly. "I believe that we're about to be an aunt and uncle. Even though technically I'm not an aunt until we actually get married."

Luke's eyes widened as the reality of what she was telling him sank in. "What?"

"I would go find Carson and bring him here. Esme has gone into labor."

Luke shook his head. "Only her baby would be born on Valentine's Day. I'll get Carson."

"And I'll get Esme comfortable." She kissed him again. "Be careful."

"You, too. I have a feeling she's going to fight back when that pain starts to hit."

Sarah went to Esme and helped her stand, because she was bent over the scrub sink, holding the side as pains rocked through her.

"Sorry, I thought I had more time," Esme panted.

"You can't control it."

Esme cursed under her breath. "It figures, though—my kid had to come on Valentine's Day."

Sarah laughed. "I know, but let's get you to a birthing room and wait for Carson to come."

Sarah walked Esme down the hall and tried not to think about the fact that in nine months she might be walking down this very same hall, with Esme holding her up, and she couldn't help but wonder what Luke was going to think when she told him, because that was something they'd never talked about in their year together.

She'd been going to tell him but then Esme had gone into labor.

Right now their conversation would have to wait, but pretty soon she wouldn't be able to hide it any longer.

"Come on, one more push." Carson was behind Esme, holding her shoulders, and Luke was pacing by the door.

"Stop pacing," Esme shouted over her shoulder. "It's annoying me."

"Sorry," Luke mumbled.

"Come on, Esme. Ignore him and give me one more push."

Esme used some choice curse words that were directed at Carson, but she gave it that one last push and soon Sarah was catching Carson and Esme's baby girl in her hands. The baby didn't even need a back rub; she began to cry lustily.

"It's a girl," Sarah announced. Esme began to cry and Carson kissed her. "Carson, you want to come cut the cord?"

Carson moved toward her and Sarah tied off the cord and handed Carson the sterile scissors. He cut the cord and then took his daughter gently in his arms, bringing her to Esme, who waited for her with open arms.

"If this doesn't change your mind about Valentine's Day, Esme, I don't know what will," Carson teased as he kissed Esme's sweaty brow again.

Sarah's heart swelled with happiness.

She wasn't used to this kind of love, this kind of family, but she had it all here and as she glanced up at Luke she could see the wonder in his eyes as he looked down at his little niece with love.

A nurse that was on duty took the newborn to weigh

her, rub ointment in her eyes and give her a vitamin K shot. Luke did the APGAR on his niece with Carson watching over his daughter and Sarah helped Esme.

Once everything was done, the newest, swaddled, seven-pound-five-ounce member of the Ralston family was handed to Esme again.

"What're you going to name her?" Sarah asked as she gently touched the baby's head.

"Not Valentine," Esme said quickly, glaring at Luke and Carson respectively.

Sarah laughed. "Well, we'll leave you alone for a bit, but really you've come through that beautifully. You can go home in the morning if her vitals remain stable."

Carson nodded. "Thanks, Sarah."

"No problem." She washed her hands and then walked out of one of the two birthing rooms they had in Crater Lake.

"That was amazing," Luke said. "You never cease to amaze me."

"What do you think they'll name her?"

Luke laughed. "My brother's so head over heels for her and the baby, he'll agree to call her anything that Esme wants. And really that's the way it should be."

"Really?" Sarah asked. "So you wouldn't object if I called our baby something like Asterix or Cantaloupe or some other fashionable name when it comes this fall?"

Luke paused. "What?"

"I was trying to tell you, but Esme interrupted us. I'm pregnant." She waited with bated breath for his reaction, but she didn't have to wait long. Before she had a chance to tease him with other names she was in his arms and he was kissing her.

"Truly?"

She nodded. “Truly. Though I’m terrified I don’t have the best example in parents. What if I end up like them?”

“Highly doubtful.” He wrapped his arms around her. “You’ll be a great mother.”

“And you’ll be a great father.”

“I love you, Sarah.” He kissed her again and she melted in his arms. “You’re my life, I would do anything for you, but I’m not naming our baby Cantaloupe.”

Sarah laughed. “I love you, too.”

And as she kissed him again she realized that she’d found her place. She’d found herself and she was right where she needed to be, in Luke’s arms.

* * * * *

MILLS & BOON®

Hardback – February 2016

ROMANCE

Leonetti's Housekeeper Bride	Lynne Graham
The Surprise De Angelis Baby	Cathy Williams
Castelli's Virgin Widow	Caitlin Crews
The Consequence He Must Claim	Dani Collins
Helios Crowns His Mistress	Michelle Smart
Illicit Night with the Greek	Susanna Carr
The Sheikh's Pregnant Prisoner	Tara Pammi
A Deal Sealed by Passion	Louise Fuller
Saved by the CEO	Barbara Wallace
Pregnant with a Royal Baby!	Susan Meier
A Deal to Mend Their Marriage	Michelle Douglas
Swept into the Rich Man's World	Katrina Cudmore
His Shock Valentine's Proposal	Amy Ruttan
Craving Her Ex-Army Doc	Amy Ruttan
The Man She Could Never Forget	Meredith Webber
The Nurse Who Stole His Heart	Alison Roberts
Her Holiday Miracle	Joanna Neil
Discovering Dr Riley	Annie Claydon
His Forever Family	Sarah M. Anderson
How to Sleep with the Boss	Janice Maynard

0116 GEN STD HB

MILLS & BOON®

Hardback – March 2016

ROMANCE

The Italian's Ruthless Seduction	Miranda Lee
Awakened by Her Desert Captor	Abby Green
A Forbidden Temptation	Anne Mather
A Vow to Secure His Legacy	Annie West
Carrying the King's Pride	Jennifer Hayward
Bound to the Tuscan Billionaire	Susan Stephens
Required to Wear the Tycoon's Ring	Maggie Cox
The Secret That Shocked De Santis	Natalie Anderson
The Greek's Ready-Made Wife	Jennifer Faye
Crown Prince's Chosen Bride	Kandy Shepherd
Billionaire, Boss...Bridegroom?	Kate Hardy
Married for their Miracle Baby	Soraya Lane
The Socialite's Secret	Carol Marinelli
London's Most Eligible Doctor	Annie O'Neil
Saving Maddie's Baby	Marion Lennox
A Sheikh to Capture Her Heart	Meredith Webber
Breaking All Their Rules	Sue MacKay
One Life-Changing Night	Louisa Heaton
The CEO's Unexpected Child	Andrea Laurence
Snowbound with the Boss	Maureen Child

0216 GEN STD HB